ON THE
FAR SIDE OF
THE MOUNTAIN

adirondacke mountains

Helderberg mountains

The far side of my mountain

catskill mountains

tree mill

garden

meadow

Bando

mrs. strawberry's farm (mrs. Fielder)

ON THE FAR SIDE OF THE MOUNTAIN

written and illustrated by

JEAN CRAIGHEAD GEORGE

DUTTON CHILDREN'S BOOKS   NEW YORK

To Twig George Pittenger,
my inspiration for this story

Copyright ©️ 1990 by Jean Craighead George

Library of Congress Cataloging-in-Publication Data

George, Jean Craighead, Date
On the far side of the mountain/by Jean Craighead George.—
1st ed.
   p.   cm.
Summary: Sam's peaceful existence in his wilderness home
is disrupted when his sister runs away and his pet falcon is
confiscated by a conservation officer.
   ISBN 0-525-44563-3
   [1. Wilderness survival—Fiction.   2. Brothers and sisters—
Fiction.   3. Falcons—Fiction.]   I. Title.   89-25988
PZ7.G29330n   1990   CIP
[Fic]—dc20   AC

Published in the United States by
Dutton Children's Books,
a division of Penguin Books USA Inc.

Printed in U.S.A.   First Edition
10 9 8 7 6 5 4 3 2 1

Contents

IN WHICH

A Storm Breaks

This June morning is hot and humid with a haze so dense I can barely see the huge hemlock tree in which I live. I like the haze. It has erased all but the great tree trunks, making my mountaintop home as simple as it was when I first came here more than two years ago.

I lean back in the lounging chair I constructed from bent saplings held together with rope made from the inner bark of the basswood tree, and enjoy the primitive forest.

A wind rises as the sun warms the earth. The haze moves off, and I see my pond, my millhouse, and the root cellar. The first year I lived here I had only a tree, a bed, and a fireplace. But one idea led to another, and the next thing I knew, I had built myself a habitat. Things just kept evolving. Take this lounging chair, for instance. One day I replaced the old stump I sat on with a three-legged stool, and then I replaced the three-legged stool with this comfortable chair.

The people changed, too. At first I was alone. Then

my family arrived and—except for my lively sister, Alice—departed. I don't know where Alice is this morning. She was going to go strawberry picking, but the haze is too dense for that. Maybe she's sitting on the porch of her tree house talking to herself just as I am. A haze mutes not only the birds and beasts, but people, too.

As a hot dry wind clears the air, I can see Frightful, my peregrine falcon, sitting in front of the six-foot-in-diameter hemlock tree that I hollowed out for a home. Unlike the chairs and people, Frightful has not changed. She still holds her body straight up and down and her head high in the manner of the peregrine falcon. Her tawny breast is decorated with black marks; her back is gray blue; her head black. When she flies, she is still a crossbow in the sky, and she still "waits on" above my head until I kick up a pheasant or a rabbit. Then she stoops, speeding toward her prey at two hundred miles an hour, the fastest animal on earth. She almost never misses.

"Hello, Frightful," I say.

"Creee, creee, creee, car-reet," she answers. That is her name for me, "Creee, creee, creee, car-reet." All peregrine falcons call the high-pitched *creees,* but when Frightful sees me in the morning or when I return from the forest, even when she is flying high above my head, she adds "car-reet." "Hello, Sam," she is saying.

She is perched on a T-block that I covered with deer-hide to protect her feet. She lifts a broad foot and scratches her head with a curved claw on the end of a long, narrow toe.

"Creee, creee, creee, car-reet."

I call her name in her own language; I whistle three notes—low, high, low. She responds by lifting the feathers on her body, then shaking them. This is called *rousing,* which is feather talk meaning "I like you." I can't speak in feathers so I answer by imitating her love notes. I do this by pulling air through my two front teeth to make a soft, cozy sound.

Sometimes I have nightmares that she has left me. I awake in a sweat and try to reason with myself. Frightful will not leave me, I say. If she were going to do that, she would have departed last spring when I was flying her free. A wild tercel, the male peregrine falcon, passed overhead. The last of the vanishing eastern peregrine falcons breed in Greenland and Canada, and a few winter as far south as the Catskills. This one was on his way to his home in the north. Frightful playfully joined him. Together they performed the peregrine courtship dance, swooping low, zooming high, then spiralling earthward. I was scared. I thought Frightful was going to leave me. I whistled. She instantly pulled deeply on her wings and sped back. Within a few feet of my outstretched hand, she braked and alighted on my glove as softly as the fluff from a dandelion seed. "Creee, creee, creee, car-reet," she said. "Hello, Frightful," I answered happily.

Now, I whistle her name again. She turns her head and looks at me. Her curved, flesh-ripping beak looks sweet and demure when you see her head on. Her overhanging brow shades large black eyes that are outlined in white feathers. She is a gorgeous creature.

At peace with me and herself, she bobs her head as she follows the flight of a bird. I cannot see it, but I know it's a bird because Frightful's feathers tell me so. She has flattened most of them to her body while lifting those between her shoulders. "Bird," that means. "Human" is feathers flattened, eyes wide, neck pulled in, wings drooped to fly.

I get to my feet. I have daydreamed enough. While the last of the haze burns off, I weed the meadow garden and split kindling before returning to my tree.

A hot sun now filters down through the lacy needles of the hemlocks in my grove. I look for Alice, wondering what she's up to. That's how one thinks of Alice— what is she up to? She's probably gone downmountain to the farm to see that pig she talks to.

Sticks snap in the distance. Someone is coming. Frightful has clamped her feathers to her body to say that whoever it is is not a friend. Her feathers read "danger." The phoebe clicks out his alarm cry and I tense. I have learned to heed these warning signals. The birds and animals see, hear, smell, and feel approaching danger long before I do. I press my ear to the ground and hear footsteps. They are heavy: possibly a black bear.

I smell the musky scent of warning from my friend
Baron Weasel. The Baron, who was living here when I
arrived, considers himself the real owner of the mountaintop, but because he finds me interesting, he lets me
stay.

Right now he doesn't like what's coming and dives into his den under the boulder. I glance at Frightful again.

Her feathers are flattened to her body, her eyes wide, neck stretched, and her wings are lowered for flight. "Human," she is saying. I wait.

A man in a green uniform rounds the bend, sees me, and hesitates as if uncertain.

"Hello," I say aloud, and to myself: Here it comes. He's some official. I've got to go to school this fall. Dad didn't pay the taxes on the farm. Alice is up to something again.

"Do you know where Sam Gribley lives?" he asks.

"Here," I answer. "I'm Sam Gribley."

"Oh," he says and glances at my face, then my berry-dyed T-shirt, and finally, my moccasins. These seem to confuse him. Apparently he is not expecting a teenager.

Suddenly he looks over my shoulder and walks past me. I spin around to see him standing before Frightful.

"My name is Leon Longbridge," he says with his back to me. "I'm the conservation officer. You're harboring an endangered species—a peregrine falcon."

I am unable to speak.

"Keeping an endangered species carries a fine and a year's imprisonment."

"I didn't know that." He faces me.

"You should have, but since you didn't, I won't arrest you. But I will have to confiscate the bird."

I can't believe what I am hearing.

"I'll let her go," I say. "I'll turn her free." I step between my bird and the man. "Won't everything be all right if she's free?"

"No," he snaps. "I'm a falconer, too. You set her loose, and as soon as I'm gone, you'll whistle and she'll come right back." He walks up to her and places his gloved hand under her breast. She steps up on it as she has been trained to do.

With a twist of his wrist he slips a hood over her head and tightens the drawstrings with his teeth and free hand. He is a falconer, I see, and a good one. My knees feel rubbery.

Frightful sits quietly. She cannot see, so she does not move, which is the reason for a hood. If a falcon is hooded she will not bate, that is, she won't fly off your fist and hang head down by her jesses, beating her wings and hurting herself.

"What will you do with her?" I ask.

"How old was she when you got her?"

"About ten days."

"Then I can't let her go. She's imprinted on you. If you raise a bird from a chick, it thinks you're its mother and that it looks like you. Such a bird won't mate with its kind, because it sees people as its kind. Set free it is worthless as far as the perpetuation of the species is concerned. And perpetuation of the species is what protecting endangered animals is all about—to let them breed and increase their kind.

"No hunger streaks," he comments as he turns

Frightful on his fist and looks her over. "I must say, you take good care of your bird for a kid." Hunger streaks appear in tail and wing feathers if a bird does not get the right food during the time the feathers are growing in.

I am thinking what to do. Mr. Longbridge has wrapped the leash tightly around his hand and now begins to move.

I walk beside him, desperately working out a plan to save her.

I try pity. "Sir, I need that bird badly. I hunt with her. She provides food for my table."

"There's a supermarket in Delhi," he says, hurrying along. I hurry along, too.

I try politeness. "Please, sir, let her go."

"You heard me."

The sun now shines out of a hazeless sky, and I can see his face more clearly. He has bony cheeks, a long nose, and heavy brows. Dark crow's-feet mark the corners of his eyes.

I try reason. "Sir, you say you can't let her go because she won't breed. If she is useless, I might as well keep her. She's useful to me."

"She'll be bred in captivity."

"But how, if she won't mate?"

"Artificial insemination. The university has a very successful artificial breeding program for endangered birds of prey." He is holding Frightful out from his body; I reach out to grab her. He sees me move and draws Frightful against his chest. I can't reach her.

I try philosophy. "But captive birds are not really birds. A bird must be part of the landscape and sky to be complete."

"Her young will be returned to the wild," he replies. "The juveniles are hacked to freedom."

He really is a falconer. *Hack* is an old falconry term. Trainers put young unleashed birds who are just learning to fly and hunt on a hack board, a sort of artificial nest. They leave them there with food, just as the parents do at the nest. The youngsters, falconers say, are "at hack"—free to fly and hunt. If they miss their prey, they come back to the board to eat. After a juvenile makes its first kill, the falconers leash and train it. I guess Frightful's young would be put at hack, but not jessed and leashed when they learned to hunt. Instead, they would fly on and live out their lives in the wild. I ask the officer if that is so.

He ignores me, so I get in front of him and walk backwards while trying to think what to do next.

Pity didn't work. Politeness didn't work. Reason and philosophy failed. I try compassion. "I love that bird. She knows me. We are bonded. She'll die without me."

"She'll adjust. All she needs is the right food."

Walking backwards, I see the color of the officer's eyes. One is brown and the other is blue. I am so fascinated that I lose the perfect opportunity to cut Frightful free, because, in spite of the hood, she bated and hung down, exposing her jesses. But I saw too late.

The officer puts his hand under Frightful's breast and returns her to his fist.

I move closer.

About three inches of leash is exposed. I whip my hunting knife from my pocket and lunge to cut it.

A karate blow to my wrist doubles me over and I stagger backwards.

"You're stealing my property," I shout.

"It's not yours."

"She is." Once I had the idea conservation officers were gentle people—not this one.

"You are harassing and talking back to an officer of the law," he shouts. "I can book you for that, *and* for harboring an endangered species."

We have come to the edge of my meadow, where a trail leads to the bottom of the mountain and the county road where he must have parked his car. He trots down it. I run after him.

Then I think of Alice. I'll call her. If he sees her yellow tufts of hair, her large eyes and bony arms and legs, and if I tell him her life depends on the falcon's catching food, he might make an exception of me and my bird. He would see that I need Frightful to fatten Alice. Adults always want to fatten Alice, even mean adults.

I don't call her. I know her well. If she saw what the officer was doing, she would dive and bite him as she bit the man who was stealing eggs from my old friend Mrs.

Fielder's chicken house. Then we'd really be in trouble, as we were that time. I can only threaten.

"I'm getting a lawyer," I call out.

Mr. Longbridge stops and comes up the mountain a few paces.

"You get a lawyer into this, and you'll go to jail for sure. You're violating the law. I really should arrest you, you know."

He turns and hurries down the trail. I run after him a short distance and give up. The law is the law.

I sink into my lounging chair and put my arms and head on my knees. I'm glad Alice isn't here. I don't have to tell her about Frightful. I need time to be alone.

IN WHICH
The Population Shrinks

Pushing back the deerskin door of my hemlock home, I enter the smoke and minty smelling tree hollow and slump to the pile of furs that replaces my outgrown sapling bed. I put my face down to cry, but no tears come.

After a long while I get up. I have to provide for Alice and myself. I should be making a box trap to catch rabbits, or a deadfall to take a deer. I don't move to do either, for I have no spirit for the jobs. It's almost as if

I am completely helpless without Frightful. I guess I am, so I had better do something to keep myself going.

Walking to my desk, I sit down at the table I built for writing. I look at my clay fireplace, which I now use only for heat and cheeriness, not cooking. I made an elaborate stone stove and oven outside where I bake, grill, and boil.

Stoves, tables, clay fireplace—I keep filling my head with thoughts about these things so I won't think about Frightful.

Reading always clears my mind; I'll try that.

I open my journal, a handsome leather-bound notebook Miss Turner gave me last summer. She said the birch-bark scrolls I used when I first came to the wilderness were too fragile for notes, but I still have them and they are as good as ever.

I thumb through the first pages hoping to find something to distract me, like a sketch of a snare, when I notice gaps in the June entries of last year. Wondering why, I begin reading the June 27 entry.

"Alice, my sister who is two years younger than I am, is going to live on the mountain with me—for better or worse.

"The way I look at it, she's here by default. Mom; Dad; my four brothers, John, Jim, Hank, and Jake; and my four sisters, Alice, Mary, Joan, and Nina climbed up my mountain three weeks ago and announced they were here to stay. Dad was going to plow the abandoned fields, sow seeds, and reap the grain. The boys said they would help build the house from the planks and two-by-fours Dad brought up here for that purpose. Mom and the girls were eager to grow a garden and keep a cow.

"Well, the house never got built. Mrs. Fielder, whom I always call Mrs. Strawberry because she and I gathered wild strawberries the spring I arrived on the mountain, was kind to my family. She offered them rooms in her large old farmhouse until they got started. She's alone and said they would be company for her.

"Hardly had my father borrowed Mrs. Strawberry's horse, Slats, and the plow, and taken them up one side of my meadow and down again, than he knew why his grandfather had abandoned this land. He was not plowing soil. He was plowing rocks. Mrs. Strawberry put it this way. 'If you want to grow stones, Mr. Gribley, this is the place for you. Here in these mountains, stones are our best crop.'

"Next Dad tried to put in a garden. After hours of digging to find soil in my meadow, he gave up. As a last resort he called in a soil conservation officer and conferred with him.

" 'The land's good for trees and wildlife,' he told Dad, 'and maybe a few wild plants that like poor soil—and that's about all.'

"June seventeenth he and Mother climbed the long, hard mountain trail to my home. One look at their faces told me they had not come for sumac tea."

I chuckle as I remember Dad asking me where Alice was—she spent most of her time up here with me—and I told him she was at the spring fiddling with a gadget she had been working on for days.

"Children," Dad said when Alice came down from the spring, "pack up your things. We're going to leave. It's impossible to farm this mountain. Men more skilled than I have tried and failed. If they couldn't do it, it's insane for me to think I can. I'm going back to what I am good at—working on the docks near the sea."

"Well, I'm not going," Alice replied nicely but firmly.

The irises in Alice's eyes look as if they are made of little pieces of blue and white crystal. When she's excited, each piece sparkles. They flashed until I thought they would splinter and crack when she told Dad she wasn't going back to the city.

"I love it here!" she said. "I'm going to stay."

"Indeed, you're not," he answered, much to my relief. I really didn't want to be responsible for a thirteen-year-old. "You're coming back to the city with Sam and the rest of us."

"Is Sam going back?" She turned to me incredulously.

"Of course," Dad answered without thinking. He hesitated. "You will, won't you, Sam?"

"No, sir," I answered. "I don't think I will. I'm doing very well here and love it."

Alice ran to Mother. "Please, let me stay," she whined like a lost puppy.

Mom walked off to think, made up her mind, and came back to me.

"Alice can stay, Sam," she said, "if you think you can support another person. She is far safer here than in the city."

My heart plunged to my toes. This is my home, my mountain, the world I had created all by myself. I needed a little sister like Frightful needed vegetables.

"What about Alice's education?" my father asked, not liking the idea either.

"She can go to correspondence school." Mother answered so promptly that it seemed that she had given this more thought than was apparent at first.

"If kids can live on sailboats going around the world," she said, "and get a good education through correspondence schools, so can Alice."

Dad could not come up with another objection. When Mother had said Alice would be safer in the woods with me than out on the mean streets, she had won.

"But for one year only," he said. Then he winked at me. "Don't worry," he whispered behind his hand. "She won't be here long. Alice gets homesick. She'll be crying like a lamb by tomorrow, and you can bring her home."

In a louder voice he said, "I'm leaving my toolbox and tools at Mrs. Strawberry's for you. I won't be needing them."

"Neither will I," I answered. Tools meant change to me, and I liked my home the way it was.

I should have been proud and happy to know my parents had so much confidence in me that they would leave Alice in my charge, but the truth was that I was peeved. Alice is not your ordinary kid. She can be wonderful company, but—she can also be Alice.

Then Mother and Dad hugged us and promised to write. As I watched them go, I felt a pang of sorrow. Not Alice. They were hardly out of sight before she blew out a breath so long it sounded as if she had been holding it for a year.

With Mom and Dad's farewells still resounding in our ears, Alice took out her Swiss Army knife, with all the gadgets on it—from screwdriver to scissors—and clipped a broken nail. Next, she pulled her socks over her knotty calves, straightened up, and smiled at me.

"Thanks, Sam," she said. "You've just made me the happiest girl in the world." Her eyes crackled.

"And now to finish my plumping mill."

"Your what?"

"I'm making a plumping mill."

"And what is *that*?"

"A plumping mill is a mechanical device run by water power. It lifts a hammer and drops it."

"And?"

"And pounds grains and nuts into flour. I'm tired of grinding acorns, Sam, I really am. So I'm making a machine that will do it for me."

"Where did you learn about a plumping mill?"

"From your librarian friend, Miss Turner, where else? I told her how hard it was to pound acorns into flour for our pancakes; she told me that the first settlers ground their grains with plumping mills."

I was intrigued. "Go on."

"She found a diagram of a plumping mill in one of her books, and I copied it down on paper then made it—come here—I'll show you."

We climbed to the cascade that spills out of the spring, and Alice picked up a four-foot sapling. On one end she had tied a rock, on the other end, a wooden box cut low on one side like a scoop. Two forked limbs, cut and trimmed, had been pounded into the ground near the cascade. A heavy stick lay across them. On top of this Alice laid the sapling on which the box and stone were fastened. She pushed the box under the cascade and arranged the stone so that it was resting on a disc of wood.

The box filled with water, became heavier than the stone, fell, and the stone went up in the air. The box emptied and, now lighter than the stone, went up. The stone plunged down and hit the wood with a thump.

"This is stupendous," I said. But Alice was not smiling, in fact, she was nearly in tears.

"No, it isn't," she wailed. "The sapling creeps off the stick all the time. I have to sit here and hold it on. I might as well pound the acorns myself for all the time it saves."

I kneeled down by the plumping mill and studied it. "This'll work," I said, seeing the problem. "It'll work just fine." I took out my knife.

While Alice sniffed and wiped tears, I carefully bored a hole through the sapling to which the stone and hammer were attached, then slipped the cross stick into the hole half way. When it balanced, I put the stick in the forks.

"Oh, Sam, that's it. You've done it," Alice said, clapping her hands. "Of course, I remember now. The sapling had a hole in it." She put a handful of boiled acorns on the disc of wood into which she had chipped a bowl. I waded into the stream and stacked the rocks on the cascade to direct the water more forcibly into the box. It filled quickly. The stone went up, the box went down, emptied, and went up. The stone crashed down. The acorns smashed. We had a plumping mill.

Alice and I sat on the bank leisurely watching as the contraption went up and down, up and down, turning acorns into flour.

"Alice," I said. "You've given me a great idea. I'm going to make a water mill. The spring puts out gallons and gallons of water an hour. If I make a dam here," I walked off a line downhill of the spring, "it will fill up this dip in the hill and we'll have a pond almost a quarter-acre big. Water from it would turn a waterwheel. The waterwheel would turn gears. Gears would run saws up and down, and I wouldn't have to cut wood an hour every day.

Alice's plumping mill

"Come on," I said, jumping to my feet. "Let's make a water mill!" I started off to get the lumber once meant for Dad's house, but Alice was not budging. She stood still with her hands on her hips.

"Don't you want to?" I asked.

"First of all I want a house."

"A house?" I said.

This young lady, I realized, was not planning to cry and go home tomorrow.

"Yes," she answered, "a house. I need a place to live. There's not enough room in your tree for me."

"I can sleep outside."

"No, I want a house up in a tree—a tree house, and I want windows and a mirror."

"A mirror?" I said incredulously and wondered how far my parents had gotten.

"I've already put some of Dad's boards up in the big oak tree on the other side of the knoll."

"You've what?"

"I've shoved some of his two-by-fours and a few planks into the white oak. Come see."

She led me past The Baron Weasel's den and down through the woods about fifty yards to the enormous old white oak. It had grown up in the open, probably when that side of the mountain was an Indian field, for its limbs grow horizontally to the ground, not up, as they do when a white oak grows in a forest reaching for the sun. I say Indian field, not great-grandfather's field, because the white oak, like my hemlock, is at least three hundred years old, maybe four. No Gribleys tilled the soil in those days.

As I pushed aside the mountain laurel, I saw three two-by-fours and some planks lying across several of the lower limbs of the tree. The oak, I saw, was a perfect foundation for a tree house.

Alice shinnied up a rope she had made of basswood bark, and I followed.

"It's not very safe," I said as the boards shifted under my feet. "But with Dad's tools, I can fix that."

With that statement, I was committed to change.

I made a few calculations. "With a few more planks, I can make a sturdy platform."

"And then," Alice said. "We'll do like the Ojibway Indians. We'll bend saplings from one side to the other to form a dome—a wigwam—and we'll cover it with bark, just like they did."

I stared at my young sister.

Alice's tree house

"And," she went on, drawing pictures in the air, "we'll make windows out of glass jars like the first settlers did, and carpet the floor with all those rabbit skins you have so I'll be warm in the winter."

"Anything else?" I asked sarcastically.

"Yes, a porch. And I'd love to have a weather vane on the roof."

"This kid," I had written then, "is definitely not going home soon."

IN WHICH
I Start Over

I turn the pages to find a blank page in my journal for today's events.

"June 17

"It's just a year since Alice moved in and stayed.

"And it's somewhere around three o'clock in the afternoon according to my sundial." I doodle with my pencil for a moment, then go on.

"Frightful was consficated today by the—"

I stop. Putting my arms on the desk and my head on my arms, I see my falcon going down the mountain on the conservation officer's fist.

Presently, I hear the leather hinges on the door of the root cellar squeak as Alice goes in. She doesn't seem to have noticed that Frightful is gone or she would be calling me. I am grateful. I just want to be by myself.

As I listen to Alice's footsteps pass my tree and fade along the path to her tree house, Leon Longbridge comes vividly back to mind. I hear his voice, see his blue eye and brown eye, and suddenly I think of something. Why didn't he show me his badge or some identification? I should think a person confiscating an endangered species would certainly have to show a person his authority to take the bird. Maybe he's not even a conservation officer.

"I'm going to Delhi and ask the sheriff," I say, hoping he isn't and that I can get her back.

I make preparations for the trip by filling my belt pouch with nuts and smoked venison. I never leave my mountaintop without food. Anything can happen to delay me—a twisted ankle, a storm, a trout waiting to be caught.

As I close the root cellar door, I find a piece of paper tucked in one of the leather hinges I made from my brother Jake's old belt. It's a note from Alice. She's always leaving me messages, usually not on paper but in the mud, written in pine needles, or scratched on a leaf. Once she floated a birch-bark note downstream to me while I was fishing.

"I'm thinking waterfalls," this one reads.

That's Alice—tantalizing—"thinking waterfalls." I'm sure she is. Ever since she set foot in the Catskills, she has talked about, and gone out of her way to find, cascades, cataracts, waterfalls, rills, riffles and niagaras.

For whatever reason she's thinking about waterfalls now, I'm glad she is. She's preoccupied and I don't have to tell her about Frightful yet.

I'll tell her in a note. That won't be as difficult as saying it to her face. I won't have to see the sorrow in her eyes or be witness to what she might do.

I return to my desk and tear a sheet out of my journal.

"Dear Alice," I begin.

"It is easier for me to write this than tell it to you. Frightful has been confiscated by the conservation officer. She's an endangered species, and the laws concerning her are rigid. I'm going to Delhi to see if there is anything I can do to get her back. I don't think there is, but it will make me feel better.

"Keep the charcoal going under the fish on the smoking rack. Turn them once more. They ought to be done by late afternoon. Wrap them in maple leaves and store them in the grape vine basket in the root cellar.

Hastily, Sam."

I leave the note on the path to her tree house, check the door on the sluice that carries the water to the waterwheel to make sure it's tightly closed, and depart.

The course I run is straight down the mountain to the county road, where I leave the cool shelter of the woods and trot over the hot asphalt to town. The traffic increases as I near the bridge over Delhi Creek, so I slow

down. The heat and stench of exhaust from the cars is
almost unbearable and I want to turn back. I don't. I
have to know.

Walking here on the streets, I feel conspicuous in my
mountain clothes, but I guess I'm not. The summer visi-
tors in Delhi are dressed in old pants and T-shirts, too.
I look no stranger than any of them in my moccasins
and the jeans my brother Jake gave me when he left.
Once I was laughed at when I wore my deerskin clothes
to town, but in these clothes no one even notices me.
And I wouldn't care if they did. I want to find Leon
Longbridge.

I round a corner and pause. The library is to the left,
the Delaware county courthouse and sheriff's office are
to the right. I strike out for the sheriff's office.

Inside a woman is working at a typewriter. Above the
door to another room is a sign reading COUNTY SHER-
IFF'S OFFICE, and under it is a card saying *Conservation
Officer on duty today.* I'll soon know the truth.

"Madam?" My voice squeaks and I clear my throat.
"Madam."

"Excuse me a minute," she answers and types on.

Presently, the typing stops. The woman takes off her
glasses and smiles.

"I was wondering, madam," I begin, then hesitate as
I try to word this just right. "I was wondering, is Mr.—
Do you have a conservation officer by the name of Leon
Longbridge?"

"Leon Longbridge?" She is scratching a mosquito bite on her neck, and my heart skips a beat, for she looks as if she has never heard of him.

"Oh, yes," she says. "Leon Longbridge is the environmental conservation officer. He just happens to be here today. He has a big territory to cover, so he's usually in the field. You're lucky."

"Can he confiscate an endangered species if somebody has one?"

"Yes, indeed, he can. He can even make arrests. Do you want to see him?"

I swallow hard in disappointment.

"No, thank you."

I walk slowly out the door.

Back on the sidewalk, I move fast, weaving in and out of the strolling people, barely noticing them. I am thinking over and over and over again: There is nothing I can do to get Frightful back. She is gone. She is gone.

Sam, I say to myself as I start across the bridge, you must stop these thoughts and start thinking about what to do now that you have no falcon.

Life, my friend Bando once said, is meeting problems and solving them whether you are an amoeba or a space traveller. I have a problem. I have to provide Alice and myself with meat. Fish, nuts, and vegetables are good and necessary, but they don't provide enough fuel for the hard physical work we do. Although we have venison now, I can't always count on getting it. So far this

year, our venison has been only road kill from in front
of Mrs. Strawberry's farm.

I decide to take the longest way home, down the flood
plain of the West Branch of the Delaware to Spillkill,
my own name for a fast stream that cascades down the
south face of the mountain range I'm on. I need time to
think. Perhaps Alice and I should be like the early Es-
kimos. We should walk, camp and hunt, and when the
seasons change, walk on to new food sources. But I love
my tree and my mountaintop.

Another solution would be to become farmers, like
the people of the Iroquois Confederacy who once lived
here. They settled in villages and planted corn and
squash, bush beans and berries. We already grow
groundnuts in the damp soil and squash in the poor
land. But the Iroquois also hunted game. I can't do that
anymore.

I'm back where I started from.

Slowly I climb the Spillkill. As I hop from rock to
rock beneath shady basswoods and hemlocks, I hear the
cry of the red-tailed hawk who nests on the mountain
crest. I am reminded of Frightful and my heart aches.
I can almost hear her call my name, Creee, creee, creee,
car-reet.

Maybe I can get her back if I plead with the man who
is in charge of the peregrines at the university. "But it's
the law," he would say. I could write to the president of
the United States and ask him to make an exception of

Alice and me. That won't work. The president swore to uphold the Constitution and laws of the United States when he took office.

I climb on. I must stop thinking about the impossible and solve the problem of what to do now. I must find a new way to provide for us. Frightful is going to be in good hands at the university, and she will have young.

I smile at the thought of little Frightfuls and lift my reluctant feet.

When I am far above the river, I take off my clothes and moccasins and bathe in a deep, clear pool until I am refreshed and thinking more clearly. Climbing up the bank, I dress and sit down. I breathe deeply of the mountain air and try to solve my problem more realistically.

Alice and I could raise chickens—no, they're domestic birds and wouldn't look right in the wilderness—pheasant and quail would be better. I put my elbows on my knees and hold my head in both hands. I don't like that idea either. Alice would undoubtedly name them and then we couldn't eat them. You can't eat pets. Alice named that pig she talks to, and now the man who owns it can't butcher it.

Across the rushing stream grows a carpet of dark moss. I wade over to it and lie down in its cool greenery. I can't go back to Alice just yet. I'm not ready to talk about Frightful. I'm just not. I close my eyes.

The leaves above me jangle like wind chimes. The vireos twitter as they carry food to their nestlings. A squirrel family scampers over the leaves, rattling them noisily, which is one of the ways squirrels communicate with each other. It means "I've found a nut crop."

The birdcalls grow more frenzied as twilight approaches. The males are making their last territorial annoucements before darkness falls. The tree frogs start singing, and I open my eyes. I am looking up into the trees.

A limb just above me resembles a shotgun.

"I would never use a gun," I say out loud. I would be forever tied to stores for bullets, and the friendly spirit of my mountaintop would be violated. The birds would not come and sit on my hand, Baron Weasel would move out, and Jessie Coon James would no longer trust me. Something happens to a person when he picks up a gun, and the animals sense it. They depart.

"No guns," I say.

In frustration I pick up a stone and throw it. It flies down the rocky stream bed and forcibly cracks against a boulder.

"Stones," I say. "I'll make a sling."

A sling is the answer. I jump to my feet. Ammunition lies everywhere, and the birds and beasts are not afraid of stones.

No sooner do I solve one problem than I face another. How do you make a sling? Not a slingshot, the forked stick with an elastic band attached to it, but the powerful sling with which David killed Goliath.

I try to remember the pictures I've seen of huge Goliath falling to earth with little David standing beneath him, his sling at his side. I see a short strap with two long cords fastened to both ends. That's all there was to it, I think, also recalling the sling my uncle made when I was a kid. To operate it, a stone is put in the strap; the ends of the strings are held and whirled above the head. When the stone is speeding, it is aimed, one string is released, and the stone zings to its mark.

I should go to the library and ask Miss Turner for a book on how to make a sling, but I can't. I don't want to tell her about Frightful. I don't want to tell anyone.

I find a basswood tree, take out my knife, and cut off several branches. Peeling off the inner bark, I braid it into a tough but slender rope. When I get home, I'll replace the bark rope with rawhide, as that will be more durable. Meanwhile I can practice.

It's almost dark when I fasten two cords to a strap of leather I cut from one of my moccasins. I swing the sling, aim at a tree, and let go. The stone misses by yards.

I think about Alice. I really should get back and tell her; she is the one who will be affected the most by Frightful's confiscation. She may even have to go home to our parents. I get to my feet and start out but sit down again. Alice will cry, or worse, she'll run down the mountain to find Leon Longbridge—and who knows what she'll do then. I think of the merchant who took Slats, the horse, because Mrs. Strawberry hadn't

paid a bill. Alice followed him to the county road and called "Kidnapper!" to the driver of a car that came along. The driver pulled over and stopped. While the merchant was trying to explain himself, Alice got on the horse and rode him back to Mrs. Strawberry.

But I can't face Alice. I'll just spend the night out here. She'll be all right even if I don't come back for days. She has enough food in the root cellar to last a long time, and if she doesn't want to eat smoked fish or venison, she can catch a fresh fish in the millpond. I caught and released some largemouth bass and a batch of bluegills in the pond shortly after it was built. They are big fish now, and Alice is good at fishing. She also knows where the yellowdock and mustard greens grow in case she wants fresh vegetables. I really don't worry about her; she's very resourceful.

As a matter of fact, she probably won't even miss me. When she's working on a project, she gets so involved she doesn't bother to come to my tree for meals. Instead she takes food from the root cellar to her tree house and works while she eats. I didn't see her for two days when she was making a mirror out of a windowpane and some mercury. When I realized she had not bought the mercury but gotten it out of a thermometer she had taken from Mr. Reilly's barn, I made her buy a new one for him with some of the forty dollars I had brought with me from the city and never spent.

When she took it back, she was so embarrassed she could hardly lift her head. Mr. Reilly was very nice about it. He said that he had done something like that when he was a kid.

"Unfortunately," he had said, "most of us have to learn from mistakes. But we do learn. I'll bet you never do this again."

"I won't," Alice had said softly. And I know she never will.

Come to think about it, if anyone is all right tonight, Alice is. Frightful must be terrified and I am miserable, but Alice, I'll bet, is humming and working and probably hasn't even read my note.

I focus on a tree trunk across the stream, twirl the sling over my head, and let a stone fly. I miss again. Discouraged, I lie down on the leafy ground and look up through the foliage at the silent moon.

IN WHICH

A Trade Comes My Way

"*Midday, June 20*

"I'm back. I stayed on the Spillkill three nights practicing with the sling and grieving for Frightful. I got one squirrel, which I brought home to eat. I missed forty times. Not good."

"Hall-oo, the tree! Hall-oo the house!"

It's Bando. I blow out my deer-fat candle and run outside to meet this old friend who is trudging up the trail.

"Hall-ooooo," I shout. I am always glad to see Bando. He's a wonderful guy. During my first year on the mountain he would hike up the steep trail and spend holidays with me. He teaches English in a college near the Hudson River, and during the long school vacations he helped me with difficult chores, like making clay pots and blueberry jam. During those days I got to know and admire him. Furthermore, he understood that I wanted to live on my own in the wilderness to test my skills and to learn. He also understood that I didn't want anyone to know where I was, because I would undoubtedly be shipped home. He never told anyone. And he was always encouraging, especially when I thought I could not make it through the blizzards of winter to spring.

Bando fell in love with this mountain that year and last spring he bought a cabin on the dirt road about two miles down the mountain from here. Three weeks later he married. His wife, Zella, is a lawyer. She's a pretty lady and I like her. She's not crazy about the cabin, however. It has no electricity or running water. The only heat comes from the fireplace. The log walls are chinked with bark and clay to keep out the cold, but they don't do the job when the wind blows hard.

When they moved in, the floor was earthen. It's one of the original cabins of the Westward Movement and, like the Iroquois Indians, the pioneers put furs down for floors, not boards. One day after Zella had swept the floor to make it look neat and clean, she picked up a stick and drew a rug of flowers, deer, and butterflies in the earth. Bando was so pleased that he told her he wasn't going to make the oak-plank floor he was planning.

That afternoon he came up the mountain to tell me he didn't understand Zella. "Her rug drawing was so wonderful," he said, "that I didn't want to cover it with a wooden floor. I thought I was complimenting her, but she turned on her heel and walked out the door. Did I miss a point?"

"Yes," I said. "She wants a floor."

Smiling as I recall that day, I join him at the top of the last steep ascent.

"Sam, I'm glad you're home." At the water mill door he drops several small logs on top of others he apparently carried up earlier. "I came by this morning, but no one was here."

"Not even Alice?" I realize I haven't seen her since I came home.

"Not even Alice."

"Maybe she's down at the library reading about waterfalls," I say. "The last I heard from her she said she was 'thinking waterfalls.'" Bando raises an eyebrow.

"Watch out, Sam. When Alice is thinking, things happen."

I smile, but not wholeheartedly.

"Sam," Bando says, pointing to the logs, "I need to saw these lengthwise—down the middle from tip to base."

"What are you making?"

"You know those two chairs I put together when you were making your chaise longue?" I nod. He and I had a good time finding limbs that were twisted and bent by the wind, the sun, and the ice. And we had a good time fashioning them into arms and legs for chairs.

"Listen to this," Bando says. "A man saw them in front of my cabin and offered me so much money for them, I couldn't refuse. He said they were fine examples of Adirondack furniture."

"What's Adirondack furniture?"

"Furniture made with the unpeeled branches and crooked forks of trees. The bark is kept on to give them that rustic look. We left it on for the same reason, but we didn't know we were stylish. Adirondack furniture was very popular at the turn of the century when people were passionate nature lovers. And, suddenly, now it is popular again."

"A man bought them, you say? Paid money for our twisted armrests and crooked chair legs?"

"Yes, and he paid a lot. I thought I'd make some more."

Bando has just showed me another solution to my problem. I can make Adirondack furniture and sell it. If I can't get enough meat with my sling, I can, and may have to, earn money. I cringe at the thought of shopping, then remember Alice likes stores.

"Want to join me in this trade?" he asks.

"I'll help you, Bando. It would be fun," I say. "But I don't want a business."

I think of Frightful and pick up one of Bando's sapling logs and concentrate on it to erase her from my mind.

"Open the sluice gate," I tell him. "I'll take the pins out of the wheel and get the saw lined up."

"Good," he says. "The sooner we get going the better. Zella wants an outdoor chair again so she can sit and look at the mountains. She's somewhat miffed that I sold her chair out from under her, as she puts it." He winks and both of his black eyebrows rise to meet his cap of white hair.

I carry a log inside the millhouse and place it against the saw, which is held in place vertically by a strong wooden frame that Bando and I made after he visited a waterwheel sawmill on the other side of the Hudson.

With a jerk of my wrist, I pull out the pins that keep the wheel from turning when not in use. It's balanced so well that when Jessie Coon James climbed up on it one day, she was carried around twice before she let go and fell in the water. After that, I locked it with pins.

"Let her roll!" I shout and look out the window.

Bando is coming down the pond hill. He passes Frightful's empty perch without noticing she's gone. I am grateful. I still can't bring myself to talk about her.

In minutes I hear the water gushing down the sluice-way, bubbling and chortling along until it spills out the end and strikes the paddles of the wheel just forward of its highest point.

It turns. I grin as I always do when I start up the mill. Water is so wonderful. It takes such a very little flow to build up enough weight to turn a big wheel and generate enormous power.

I put my elbows on the windowsill while Bando saws. Not seeing any sign of Alice, I begin to wonder seriously what she's doing. Maybe she's working on another one of her "great ideas." I hope not. They can be humdingers. Last autumn when the waterwheel was still under construction, Alice came to my tree while I was trying to figure out where to dig an irrigation ditch to carry the water from the millpond to the squash and groundnuts in the rocky meadow. I was concentrating on one of the maps the correspondence school had sent her for a course in map reading and mapmaking. My mountain and all its elevations were on it, so I was studying the contours for the waterway when she stuck her head in the door.

"Sam," she said. "Look at this."

"Alice, please. I'm working."

"But this is important. Really important. The correspondence school is offering a science course."

I lost my concentration and irritably put down my pencil and stepped outside. "Alice, what *do* you want?"

"Sam, the first lesson is how to convert a water mill to electricity. Let's make electricity when we finish the mill."

"I don't want electricity, Alice."

"We could have electric heaters. I can't write well with mittens on."

"I don't want electric heaters. I like the fire."

"Sam, you're just an old fogy. I'm going to take that course. I'll make electricity if you won't."

"No, Alice, no. I will not have electricity on my mountain."

"Sam," her eyes crackled. "This is my mountain, too. The farm belongs to Mr. and Mrs. Charles Gribley, who happen to be my parents as well as yours." She looked right into my eyes and clamped her jaws tightly. "You have no right to stop me from doing what I want to do in my own home!"

"Maybe not," I said. "But nevertheless, I don't want electricity and all that it will bring—radios, TV, vacuum cleaners, hair dryers, washing machines—noise. I want to hear the birds."

In her disgust Alice pulled off her rabbit-lined hat so fast it created static electricity in her hair. The yellow wisps stood up on end like a circus clown's, and I wondered how I ever thought she was cute.

"Sam?" Bando's voice snaps me out of my daydream. He is staring at me. "Are you all right? You're glassy-eyed."

"I'm not all right, Bando," I answer, the image of my regal bird flashing into my mind. "Frightful was confiscated by the conservation officer three days ago." I almost break down but regain my composure and go on. "I should have told you when I first saw you, but I just couldn't."

He sits down on a block of wood.

"Is that really true?"

"Yes, it is."

"That's dreadful." Bando runs his fingers through his hair. "I've been afraid of this. Zella brought me a copy of the Endangered Species Act not long ago. I should have told you about it, but I thought the conservation officer understood your needs."

I am fighting back tears now. "It's all right." I bite my lower lip. After a while I am able to tell him about Leon Longbridge and how he is taking Frightful to the university to be bred. He listens.

"I think she'll die without you, Sam."

"Oh, no," I say, trying to be convincing. "She's a bird. She'll eat and thrive."

We saw Bando's logs without any more words.

"What are you going to do, Sam?" he asks when we are done. "I mean how are you going to live?"

"I made a sling." I take it from my pocket.

"Are you any good at it? That's a tough martial art to master."

"I'm not very good at it."

Bando puts most of the slats in his packbasket and stacks the others in the corner of the millhouse, to collect later.

"If you ever want a job in my furniture factory . . ." he says, but stops in mid-sentence. He has no heart for facetiousness.

Shouldering his packbasket, he leaves the millhouse.

I climb to the millpond, close the gate, and watch the water slow down, trickle, and then stop. I finger the sling in my pocket.

IN WHICH
I Go Backwards in Order to Go Forwards

When Bando left, I opened my journal again. Since reading about the old days keeps my mind off Frightful, I flip to last summer and the days when we were building the dam and water mill. Those were wonderful times.

The water mill was begun soon after the plumping mill.

The dam came first. After I had gathered enough roots and bulbs and smoked enough fish to last Alice and me for a couple of months, I began it. Then I waded into the stream that comes from the spring and began to stack logs, stones, and mud where I had planned the dam the day our folks left. Little did I know it wouldn't last.

"*July 29*

"A big storm dumped so much water on the mountain the last three days that the dam washed out—logs, rocks, and mud.

" 'Now what do we do?' " I asked Alice.

" 'The beaver dam didn't wash out,' she said. 'I saw it this morning when I was picking raspberries. Let's go see what they do right.' "

"Later That Night

"At twilight I climbed a tree and watched a pair of young beavers begin a new dam. They started it not with the big logs and rocks I had used but with shrubs and saplings placed butt-ends upstream. As soon as a low spot developed and the water ran out, they blocked the flow with sticks. This gradually raised the height and raised it evenly."

"August 15

"Alice and I did as the beavers did and we have a dam.

"Right away, our dam leaked, so down the mountain I went to see how the beavers made theirs watertight. They carried mud on their flat tails and plastered it on the upstream side of the dam. The current washed the mud in among the sticks and stones and sealed the leaks. I had been plastering holes on the downstream side of the dam where I saw the leaks. Naturally, this mud washed out. So back I went and mended my dam like the beavers did. It worked.

"When I was finished, we had an extraordinarily strong dam, which, like the beavers', was much wider at the base than the top. This counteracts the immense pressure on the bottom of the dam. Today we have a quarter-acre pond which already has frogs and little fish. I'm going to stock it with bass and bluegills."

The millhouse came next.

"August 21

"There are stones everywhere on this mountain, as Dad well knows, and so it seemed sensible to make the millhouse out of stones. The rocks are sandstone and shale, which were laid down layer upon layer in an ancient sea that existed before the mountains rose. The shale, in particular, breaks into perfect building blocks with the tap of the hammer in the right place. I got real good at this and, within the week, had a pile of stones ready to be stacked into a millhouse.

"I met Miss Turner one day while I was hunting Frightful and told her about the project. The next day she came up the mountain with a book on how to build dry walls—no mortar—just stones."

I wrote this in my journal.

"Lay the stones level, that's the first principle in keeping a wall from shifting and falling down.

"The second is to lay the stones one on two, two on one.

"Our great grandfathers built stone walls and buildings that are standing today. In Europe some have been standing since the year 1000."

"September 14

"The millhouse is done. It stands below the dam on that flat spot the stream carved before it took its present course down the mountain. It looks very natural there, and as soon as the mosses take hold, it will look even more so. One door, one window, and a hole for the shaft are all the openings we built, because they are very difficult to make. The window, however, lets in lots of light, and I'll be able to see just fine when I work.

"The millhouse looks very professional thanks to Miss Turner. She read the how-to books carefully and was very fussy about which stones she put where. She took her vacation up here so that she could supervise the laying of the walls. She also gave all of us work gloves. Stones are hard on your hands.

"Mrs. Strawberry came up one day and tapped stones. She was a master at it, breaking them into almost perfect blocks. She got way ahead of the builders—Alice, Miss Turner, and me—so we got Bando and Zella and they gladly pitched in.

"This is the first time I've seen Zella happy on the mountain. She had been taught by her grandfather, a bricklayer, how to make corners when she was a kid, and she was delighted to see how much she remembered. The corners, as well as the walls, are very professional and strong because of Miss Turner and Zella."

"*September 15*

"Zella went off on a law case, and Bando stayed here to help with the millhouse roof. We decided not to put on a gabled roof right now, because we want to make the sluice, the trough that carries the water from the pond to the mill. So the roof is just logs covered with bark to keep out the rain."

"*September 28*

"The sluice is in place. Getting it there was fairly easy, for I simply felled the big hemlock at the edge of the pond. Mrs. Strawberry showed me how to drop the tree right where I wanted it.

"She notched it with Dad's axe in the direction I had marked for it to fall—from the dam to the millhouse— and then she told me to saw on the opposite side. After an hour or so I heard the tree snap. It tilted, began to fall slowly, then faster and faster until it crashed down with a splintering of limbs to lie exactly where Mrs. Strawberry had said it would. She wiped her hands, saying she should have been a lumberjack.

"I knew I had to burn and chip out the inside of the tree to make a trough, like the pioneers made water pipes. It was not hard work, but it was a tedious chore I could do when I didn't have help, so Bando and I started on the waterwheel."

"October 10

"Bando had a Columbus Day vacation and helped collect the last of Dad's house lumber. Then we borrowed Slats to haul the planks from the collapsed barn on Bando's property. With a carpentry compass, I drew a huge circle on the ground. This was our pattern for the wheel.

"For three days we fitted boards into the circle, and when we were finished, we had two doughnut-shaped structures six feet in diameter and fourteen inches deep. Bando will come back next weekend to help build the shaft and spokes.

"Meanwhile I'm nailing the paddleboard between the two wheels while Alice and Miss Turner are building a wall outside the millhouse on which to lay the wheel shaft. Bando had a carpenter make two bearings—large blocks of wood, each with a U in them—in which the shaft will lie and turn. One will be on the wall Alice and Miss Turner are working on, the other will be inside."

"November 25

"It's taken until today to get the waterwheel in place. Bando and Zella were too busy to come to the mountain during most of November, and Miss Turner's mother was sick, so she couldn't work. I did finish the sluice but stopped working on the wheel because Alice and I had to gather the nut crop. The beechnuts are abundant this year, and so are the hickory and butter nuts, but the acorn crop is poor. Alice did find one productive tree, and we have enough to last until spring.

"Work was further delayed when Mrs. Strawberry came up to tell us that another deer had been killed on the county road and I went down to butcher that prize and haul it up here.

"Then the smoking of the venison took more time. While I was working at that, Alice decided to make a smokehouse, and before I knew it, she had me tapping and stacking stones again. Although it delayed the mill, I'm glad we made it. The venison is much better when smoked in a building where the fire can be controlled.

"I was delayed even further because Alice wanted rabbit skins tacked on the floor and walls of her tree house before the cold set in. To get enough, I spent extra hours hunting with Frightful each afternoon. I was almost finished with the job when, at the end of the day, I met a cousin of Mrs. Strawberry walking along the dirt road with his sheep. He's a sheepherder, and when he learned I was making my sister a carpet with the rabbit I was carrying, he offered me two sheepskins. I didn't refuse them, but Alice and I didn't use them for rugs, we made them into parkas for the winter. More time from the wheel.

"Alice has her weather vane. One day she fussed because I hadn't made her one, and so I stopped shaping the shaft for the waterwheel and went to work on the weather vane.

"All I did was fit a narrow-necked bottle snugly in a wooden box. Into the bottle I put a stick with a slit at the top, and into the slit I shoved an arrow-shaped board. I held it in place with pegs. The pegs are square. I read that if you put square pegs in round holes the wood welds and stays tight for years.

"When it was done, I climbed up on her roof and secured it with deer tendon. Then we stood on her porch admiring it.

" 'The wind is blowing from the north northwest,' said Alice clapping her hands. 'Tomorrow will be a beautiful day.'

"Actually, the weather vane has proved to be very useful, but a barometer I made has been even more so. It's a wide-mouthed Mason jar with a piece of a rubber glove Zella gave me tied securely over it. I picked a clear day to tie it on because, when you seal the jar, the air is trapped inside at the pressure of the day on which you make it. If it's a rainy day, your reading will always be low.

"When a storm is coming, the rubber cap indents to say that the barometric pressure is low. One day I saw that it was indented severely, and cancelled a foraging trip. The storm turned out to be a cloudburst, and an island where we were going to spend the night was flooded.

"So it wasn't until yesterday that Bando and I got the wheel in place with the help of Mrs. Strawberry, Slats, Alice, Zella, and Miss Turner.

"We threw a rope over a limb, tied one end to the wheel and the other to Slats. Then Mrs. Strawberry led him slowly away from the tree. The wheel rose into the air until we could push and guide it. With everyone helping, we eased the wheel to the mill and carefully directed the shaft through the hole in the streamside wall made for this purpose. Inside we laid it to rest on the bearing. Mrs. Strawberry backed up Slats, lowering the outside end of the shaft on Alice and Miss Turner's stone wall. With that, the waterwheel was in place.

"Alice ran to the pond and opened the sluice gate. The water rolled down the hollowed tree, hit the wheel blades—and the darn thing turned. We cheered and clapped and danced. We had a rolling waterwheel!"

"November 29

"We had wonderful feast day on Thanksgiving. Miss Turner brought up a turkey, and Mrs. Strawberry and Zella made salad and pumpkin pie. Alice and I baked acorn bread in my stone oven. The day was warm, and we ate outside watching the waterwheel turn. We all felt great pride and satisfaction."

"November 30

"But a turning wheel does not do anyone much good. The shaft has to turn something to be useful. So I made a cog wheel or gear out of a disc of oak by putting pegs around the edge.

"I fitted the cog wheel onto the shaft and made a smaller cog wheel to fit into the pegs of the first. Into the smaller one I inserted a bent iron to which I attached Dad's saw in the frame. I would sure like to try to run the saw, but I'll wait for my friends. They're all coming next weekend for the big moment."

"December 6

"Everybody gathered for the opening of the sawmill. Miss Turner made the bread this time, Bando and Zella brought cheese, and Mrs. Strawberry made corn pudding. Alice had brewed some tea with wild peppermint

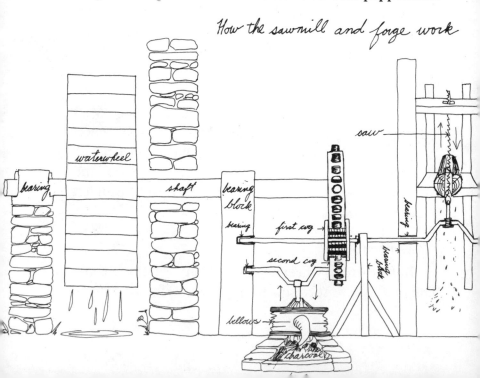

How the sawmill and forge work

leaves, and I contributed two nice bass. They grow fast in ponds.

"At high noon I held a log in front of the saw. Alice opened the sluice gate and ran back to join us faster than the water flowed.

"We cheered as it rushed forward, hit the blades, turned the wheel and shaft which turned the first cog which turned the second cog which sent the saw up and down!

"We made so much noise cheering that Frightful bated and I had to rescue her to keep her from breaking her pinions. Hearing the noise, the crows came in to see if we were harassing an owl."

I stop reading my journal and look up. The water mill was a big change. I sawed wood and made a gable for the millhouse roof and shingles to cover it. I had leaped from the Stone Age into the beginning of the Industrial Revolution without any pain, in fact, with a lot of joy.

A few days after the mill was running, Alice poked her head in the door of my tree while I was writing.

"You're not going to have acorn pancakes, Sam Gribley," she said, "unless you make a waterfall for my plumping mill."

I had forgotten all about her mill in the excitement of building the dam and sawmill. The cascade that ran her mill was now underwater. So that very day I made a staircase of stones under the pond overflow. The water splashed down, filled her wooden box and lifted the stone, and she was back in business again. The falls are attractive and sound nice in the evening. I can understand why Alice likes waterfalls.

I go back to my journal.

"Christmas Eve

"I added another cog wheel with a bent iron. To the iron I attached a bellows. I cut boards from Bando's barn siding into two heart shapes. A wide strip of deerskin pegged to each allowed them to move up and down. A cow horn made a perfect nozzle through which the air rushed when the bellows was pumped. I laid the bellows on a low table made of stones and directed the stream of air onto the charcoal in a stone fire bin. When the wheel turned, the third cog wheel pushed the bellows up and down, and I had a forge.

"Now I can bend and shape pieces of iron I find around the ruins of the Gribley house and barn. Eventually I'll forge them into shovels, ladles, and even nails."

"Christmas Day

"This is the day of our annual Christmas party. Bando, Zella, and Miss Turner were going to join us for a wild turkey Frightful caught, but a big snowstorm struck last night, and no one got up the mountain.

"In the morning Alice fed the wild birds and I dug down to Baron Weasel's den to see what he was up to. As I was tunneling in to him, he was tunneling out to me. He burst out of the snow and slid down the hill on his belly.

"One fellow I don't have to worry about in a snowstorm is The Baron Weasel. Later he arrived at my tree for Christmas dinner. I gave him the liver and giblets from the turkey."

"December 26

"The pond is a white muffin, the millhouse has disappeared under a snowdrift, and Alice and I are playing checkers with groundnuts and dried apples. Winter is here."

IN WHICH

I Am in for a Surprise

I hear the latch on the root cellar door thump and close my journal. Alice must be getting something for supper. I have put off talking to her about Frightful long enough. I get to my feet.

Stepping out of the darkness of my tree into the bright light, I squint, then walk to the cellar. No one is there.

The door is closed, and the lock, which is a board that lies across two brackets, is tilted and is almost out at one end. Someone was here, but it wasn't Alice. She's too protective of our hard-won supplies to leave the lock ajar. It must have been Jessie Coon James. She's always fiddling with this lock. In fact, I made it because Jessie once opened the door with her little handlike paws and helped herself to venison and nuts. From the looks of things, I had best make a better lock. She has this one all but figured out.

As I open the door, the clean scent of apples greets me. They came from the trees Great-grandfather Gribley planted. Even though they're now old and choked by forest, they produce plenty of apples for Alice and me.

I decide to bake a squash for supper. I feel my way to the back of this cave, which I dug into the side of the hill to keep our food dark and cool. The cattail rush basket in which we store the hickory nuts is almost empty. That's funny. Although I took some to Delhi with me, I didn't think I'd taken that many. I wonder if that raccoon of mine did get in here after all. There might be a hole in the stone wall that I faced the cave with.

I check the other supplies. The basket of groundnuts is almost empty. It couldn't be Jessie. She makes a complete shambles of the cellar when she gets in. So it must be Alice. She brought back a wild-food cookbook from the library last week and mentioned that one of the recipes called for lots of nuts.

I step over the jars of maple syrup that Alice and I made last February and pick up a squash. Alice planted

squash seeds a year ago, and they grew as big as pump-
kins—some plants like our poor soil.

After locking the door securely by wedging a stone in
the brace, I carry the vegetable to my outdoor kitchen
and start off for the tree house and Alice.

The trail to her house is bordered with stones she
gathered and put there. She wanted to edge all the
paths, but I objected. Bordered trails get too much use.
The wildflowers can't push up, and when they don't
grow, the soil erodes and is carried into the streams by
the rain. The best thing to do, I told Alice, is to take
different routes from place to place, or put a log across
an old path and let it rest. I kick leaves onto her trail to
protect it. Jessie Coon James walks up to me.

"Hello there, Jessie," I say as my old friend greets me
with a chittering purr. Gathering her up in my arms, I
give her a big hug. Gently she sticks her black paws in
my ears, feels my cheek, then turns around, and, hanging onto my neck with her hind legs, reaches down into
my pocket with her front paws. She finds the venison.

"You're real hungry, Jessie," I say. "How come?
Hasn't Alice fed you today?"

Jessie moved in with Alice when the cold weather
arrived last fall and never moved out. Raccoons sleep in
dens in the winter. Alice's dimly lit tree house was snug
and better than a hollow tree because, when she awoke
on warm days, Alice fed her. In February she left to find
a mate, but hardly had a week passed before she was
back in her tree house. In March she had four babies.

She and Alice took care of them until they were on their own.

It's unusual for Jessie to be so hungry. One thing Alice does not do is neglect animals.

As I mull all this, Jessie climbs up on my shoulder and eats the venison.

"Hey," I say, "I know what's the matter with you. Alice isn't here. And she hasn't been for several days, by your appetite."

I put her down and run up the steps, notched in a log, to Alice's front porch and push back her blanket door. The light from the Mason-jar window falls on a note lying in plain view on the furs. I have a hunch this is not one of her ordinary notes. I snatch it up. It's not dated.

"Dear Sam,
"I'm leaving. Don't worry about me. I'll be just fine thanks to all you have taught me.
Love, Alice."

I read the note twice more.

Alice has left.

I can't believe it, so I read it a fourth time, then walk out on her porch and sit down, dangling my legs in the air. She must be mad at me for not converting to electricity, or because I don't like her stone-lined paths. She might be angry about the irrigation ditch. We argued about it. She claimed it took water from her cascade and plumping mill. I insisted, in fact I thought I proved, that it didn't.

Why is she leaving? I ask myself. She can't just walk off this way.

Hey, Sam Gribley, I admonish. Didn't you pack up a few belongings, tell your father you were going to leave, and take off for the adventure of your life?

"Okay, Alice," I say out loud. "It's your turn."

In fact, Alice is better prepared to take care of herself than I was when I left home. I didn't know anything about the wilderness. She can catch fish with a thorn hook and a line of braided basswood, and she knows the wild edible plants.

I back down the steps and pick up Jessie. I am feeling very sorry for myself. Frightful has been confiscated—and now Alice is gone. Even if we did argue a lot, she was good company.

"Hall-oo, the tree!"

Bando's here! And just in time.

I run up the path, trot along the edge of the pond, then, placing my two feet together, leap goatlike down the slope to the millhouse.

"Bando!" I cry eagerly and put Jessie down.

"What's the matter with you, Sam? You act as if you haven't seen me for years. I was just here." He throws some fine crooked limbs on the ground, reaches into a pocket on his vest, and hands me a pamphlet.

"Zella sent this. Alice told her you wanted it."

"*Making Electricity with Water Mills,*" I read. "Alice said *I* wanted this?"

"Yes," Bando answers. "And Zella said to tell you that if you do get the mill generating electricity, please bring a wire down to her." He looks at me hopelessly. "She wants electric lights and an electric stove."

I barely hear him. That Alice can fight with me even when she's not here. I don't want electricity, Alice.

I stuff the pamphlet under a stone in the corner of the mill, thinking as I do so that it *is* good Alice has gone off on her own.

Bando walks to the pond and opens the sluice gate. The water gushes forward, the wheel turns, and he joins me, whistling some obscure tune. Running the water-wheel always puts him in high spirits. He picks up a contorted sapling.

"How do you like this piece for an arm?"

"It's okay," I say without much interest, for I am still arguing with Alice.

Leaving Bando at the saw, I walk back to my tree. After washing the squash in the pond, I build a fire in the stone oven I built not long after the millhouse was completed. When the fire is roaring hot, I rake the burning coals to one side, put the squash on the large sandstone slab at the bottom of the oven, and close the door. The door is another slab of sandstone.

I've decided to barbeque the squirrel to go with the squash, so I light a second fire in the pit under the grill.

This is made from long, narrow pieces of shale laid on the top of a stone-lined pit like slats on an orange crate. There's a reflector at the far end, which is another stone slab propped to throw heat on the grill. In winter it also throws heat into my tree. Tonight it's too hot for that, so I lift the reflector and lay it on the ground.

While supper cooks and the waterwheel turns, I spade the ditch that will carry the pond water to the plants in the meadow. Now and then I run back to the grill and turn the squirrel. I don't look at the path to Alice's tree house or Frightful's empty perch.

Eventually Bando climbs the hill, closes the sluice

gate, and comes to my outdoor kitchen. He sits down on a section of stump at my table, which is a huge sandstone slab laid on three big boulders. I sit across from him.

I want to tell him about Alice. I don't. She has a right to her privacy. When she's ready, she'll tell me what she's been up to.

Bando folds his hands on the table and clears his throat.

"I'm so sorry about Frightful," he says.

I can't think of what to say, so I walk over to the squirrel and turn it again. Bando sees I'm not ready to talk.

"I'll leave you to your thoughts, Sam," he says and gets to his feet.

Shouldering his packbasket, now filled with future chair arms and legs, he leaves.

Just before sundown the squash is cooked and the squirrel is juicy and tender. I serve myself on one of the wooden plates I carved when we were snowed in last winter.

Funny thing, I skipped breakfast and lunch today, but I'm not hungry. I think people have better appetites when they eat with someone, even if they argue. I give the squirrel to Jessie and put the squash in the root cellar for tomorrow.

When night comes, I do not go to bed in my tree but stretch out on my lounging chair and listen for Alice.

I thought she might get frightened and come home. I should have known better than that.

At midnight, I walk to the head of the trail that leads to the bottom of the mountain. An owl hoots; a bird sleeping in a laurel bush awakes and flutters its wings.

As I amble back, I wonder if Mrs. Strawberry knows what Alice is up to. They talk a lot, so she just might. It's not that I want to pry, but maybe Alice is not going off to find her own home. Maybe she's just down the mountain with that pig.

As I finally crawl into my tree, I wonder what she took with her. If I knew I might figure out where she's going. I light my deer-fat candle and go down the trail to Alice's tree house once more. It's a very warm night and I'm glad for that. Alice can sleep on the bare ground and be perfectly comfortable.

Inside her wigwam I see that her deerskin pants we made last spring are missing, as well as the denim jacket she came here with. Two of the four T-shirts that hung on the pegs by the door are gone. Her tennis shoes are here, but not her boots. She must be expecting rough terrain. She's not talking to a pig, then.

She's left all her books, as far as I can see, but has taken the maps from the orienteering, or map reading, course. Also gone are her backpack and our water carrier, a square of hide folded in fourths. It's a great device, because it can also be used for a pillow or a hat— all of which means she will not be back soon.

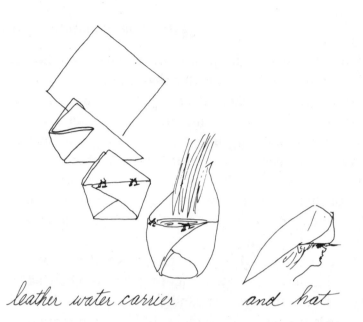

leather water carrier   and hat

I recall the nearly empty hickory nut and groundnut baskets. I didn't notice if any of the smoked venison or fish was gone, but I'll bet they are.

Her Swiss Army knife's not here, which I would expect no matter where she was going. She takes it everywhere. But why aren't her gloves on the peg? Bando said the temperature has been in the eighties by day and seventies by night. Maybe she's going to build a stone house at her new home site and needs her gloves.

As I wander back to my tree, I think of Alice alone in the forest, as I once was. I remember my frustration as I tried to start a fire the first night, and my fear when I couldn't catch a fish to eat. Then I remember the triumphs of making a fire, catching a fish, and sleeping on a bed of pine boughs all alone in the wilderness. I'm a bit envious of Alice. I'm also a whole lot curious. Tomorrow I'll ask Mrs. Strawberry if she knows where Alice went. Not that I would try to find her, but I would like to know what she's up to.

IN WHICH

I Am Sent East by Northeast

Just before sunrise I strike out across the field to Mrs. Strawberry's weatherworn farmhouse. Tucked in a grove of old lilacs, it is surrounded by barns and outbuildings that are sagging toward the ground. These mountains do not love a farm.

At the gate, Slats trots up and tries to shove his way into the yard with me.

"Phbbbbbb," I say, blowing through my lips. According to Mrs. Strawberry, this is horse talk for "You're annoying." Frightful doesn't have such a word in her vocabulary, but then her ancestors were never pestered by flies as were Slats's.

I lift the latch and push him back. He paws the ground.

"You can't come in," I say. "So stop begging." Pawing the ground is a horse's way of begging.

As I step into the yard, I glance up at my mountain. It's strong and beautiful, with the sun rising behind it.

The view from here is its western side. No matter from which direction you look, it's an inspiring sight. Why on earth would Alice want to leave?

A green frog pipes, a star shoots, and a light comes on in Mrs. Strawberry's farm kitchen. I knock.

"Sam!" she says, opening the door. "What are you doing here?" She is wearing the brown felt hat she always wears in and out of doors and is smiling her I'm-REALLY-glad-to-see-you smile. It softens the lines around her sharp nose and pointed chin.

"Come in," she says. "Have some breakfast."

Slats grabs the gate in his teeth and rattles it, then thrashes his head up and down.

"No, you can't come in, Slats!" Mrs. Strawberry calls.

"He's annoyed," she says to me. "Alice hasn't been around to ride him since she started her new project."

I hold my breath—she knows.

"Does Alice have a new project?"

"Yes, indeedy, she's up to something again."

"Do you know what it is?" I try to sound as if I were asking if Alice were in the barn pitching hay.

"Don't you?" she asks.

"No."

"I don't either. Never asked."

"She's left home—to find a new one, I think."

"My goodness," she replies. "That's quite a project."

My face must look troubled because the next thing Mrs. Strawberry says is, "Don't you worry, Sam. Whatever Alice is up to, she's all right. Go on home and do your chores."

"I'm not worried—just curious. She took her maps."

"Hmm. Sounds like she's going far."

"That's what I think. And she's got a good start. The last time I saw her was five days ago. The first day the haze rolled in. The next day I left for Delhi without seeing her. When I returned, she was gone."

"I saw her three days ago," Mrs. Strawberry says. She steps over to a flowerpot to pick off dead geraniums.

Three days ago—that means she started the day after Frightful was confiscated. I make a quick calculation. Alice and I can walk about twenty miles a day. That could put her sixty miles from here. Sixty miles, which way? in what direction?

If I knew in which direction she was going, I might be able to look at a map and figure out her destination. I'd sure like to know where she's headed.

She should have told me. At least I told Dad that I was going to run away to Great-grandfather Gribley's farm. He didn't believe me, but he should have. Alice hasn't even given me a hint—at least I don't recognize one if she has.

I linger, hoping Mrs. Strawberry's memory will keep clearing and she will remember more about "what Alice is up to," as we all say.

Slats takes the gate in his teeth and shakes it again.

"Ee-he-eeeeeee," squeals Mrs. Strawberry. She's imitating the cry of a challenging horse, like western cowboys do to discipline their steeds. Hearing a threat in his own language, Slats trots off.

"You just have to be stern with that horse," she says. "It's like Alice and her pig. She can get that pig to do anything with a stern bit of pig talk."

"*Her* pig," I exclaim. "I knew she had a pig friend, but I didn't know it was hers."

"It is now. Mr. Reilly"—she points to a farm down the road—"who owns Crystal, or who did own her, gave Crystal to her."

"That was very nice of him."

"Not really. Alice gave the pig a name so he didn't have the heart to butcher her. And the pig loves Alice. Crystal won't eat if she isn't around. Pigs are very affectionate, especially to children, and particularly to a child who learns to say, 'I love you' in pig-ese." I keep listening, my picture of Alice and her pig taking on new dimensions.

"Now that I think about it," Mrs. Strawberry goes on, "Alice might have been going off to find her own place." She draws on her memory. "She was leading her pig on a leash."

"Alice took her pig?" I smile. She can't go very fast or far with a pig, and—a pig can be easily tracked.

Of course, I'm not going to follow her, although it would be easier than playing On the Track, the game we made up when went berrying or food gathering. You track the other person by observing broken sticks or footprints or even clues that a person sets out, like an acorn under a pine tree. It's fun.

I'll just find their first few tracks and figure out where Alice is. Then I'll go home.

Mrs. Strawberry is watching me closely.

"Are you worried about her, Sam?"

"Not at all," I answer, thinking how easy it will be to find pig prints and pig droppings. She studies my face again. She doesn't believe me.

"I can't help you very much," she goes on, "but I can tell you this, she and the pig were walking across my fallow field, toward your mountain. I thought they were going home."

"South?" I ask eagerly.

"South and a little bit east." I thank her very much and hurry down the steps to the gate.

Out of sight of Mrs. Strawberry, I veer toward Mr. Reilly's house, leaping mullens and thistles growing in the fallow field. Perhaps *he* knows where Alice is going.

As I approach the lights in the cow barn, I slow down and stop. Alice is a secret-keeper among other things. If Mrs. Strawberry doesn't know, he won't know either.

Making a right-angle turn, I go south and slightly east across the field. I watch for bent grasses and hoof-prints.

At the end of Mrs. Strawberry's property, two hills meet in a swamp. Dead trees rise out of the dark water. In them are eight blue heron nests—a rookery. Eight nests, I say. That might mean sixteen more great blue herons if all goes well this summer.

I climb the fence and continue walking south and a bit east, searching for pig tracks among the rushes and trees along the swamp stream. I can't find any. You'd think a pig would leave a beaten trail in this wetland, but Crystal hasn't or, at least, I can't find it.

The haze thickens as the sun warms the land, and I can't see well so I sit on a log by the stream and wait for the air to clear.

A blue jay who flew into a willow when I sat down is right above me, a prisoner of the haze too. He doesn't see me. We both sit still and wait.

At last the wind blows, the whiteness thins, and the blue jay catches sight of me. He screams and flies over a sandy spit.

"Well, look at that!" I exclaim out loud and jump to the spit. "Alice has been here."

A stick is standing upright in the sand. Two rocks have been placed on either side of it, about three feet apart. A line has been drawn between them. Another line intersects the first.

I have found a compass made by Alice. We make these when we're travelling in strange forests. To make one, you pound a stick in the ground and put a stone at the end of its shadow. That is west. After about an hour you put another stone on the end of the new position of the stick's shadow. That is east. You draw an east-west line between the two stones, then the north-south. Alice has labeled north.

The compass is a good find, but it doesn't tell me which way she's going. I get down on all fours and look more closely to see if she has plotted her direction—and

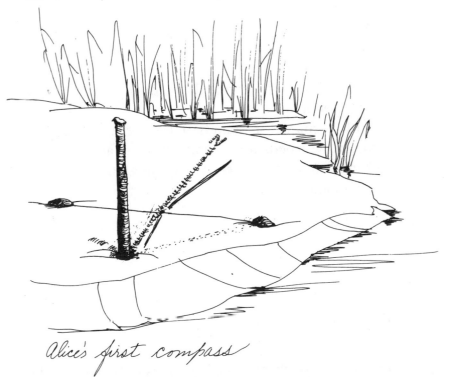

Alice's first compass

she has! Two thin reeds on the sand point from the center of the compass outward. The longest points east by northeast or about 70 degrees. The other points almost due south.

I know what she's doing. She and I use long sticks or reeds to indicate our long-range objective, short ones to point out the immediate route. She must be reading one of the maps she took. Although she's headed east by northeast for the long run, she's going almost due south for a short distance.

Alice has plotted her course. This is no exercise for her map-reading teacher; this is serious. She's off on her own—with a pig.

She knows exactly where she is going, and I will, too, before very long.

With a couple of bounds, I leave the stream, run through the woods for a short distance, and climb an embankment to the dirt road that runs along the bottom of my mountain.

IN WHICH
Zella Makes Sense

The answer to where Alice is going is in Bando's cabin. I jog up the dusty road that follows the creek. I'll soon know where she's headed. Then I'll go home and do the chores.

As I climb over the fence into Bando's pasture, a song

sparrow clicks out his alarm note from the raspberry thicket. I assume I am his enemy until I see a crow sneaking toward his nest intent upon eating the eggs. I rush the crow. He flies off, crying his alarm caws.

Bando looks up when he hears the crow and hails me. He's in front of his cabin in the shade of the big slippery elm tree, contemplating a twisted limb. Bando really *is* serious about making Adirondack furniture. He's up and at work, and the sun is hardly over the treetops.

"What brings you here, Sam?" he asks when I join him. His prematurely white hair is cut so short that it looks like a skullcap. Bando is getting a little paunch, but I like it, especially right now. He looks older and wiser, and that makes me feel better. This has been a bad week: first Frightful, then Alice.

"You look like you ate a green persimmon, Sam," he says.

"Alice ran away."

He drops the twisted wood.

"Really? Where did she go?"

"I don't know." Bando looks worried so I quickly add, "She's perfectly all right. She made a sun compass in the sand along the marsh creek to plot her direction. I'll know where she's going if I can look at your maps."

"Sure," he says. "Come on in." Bando has been collecting the same maps Alice got from her school course ever since he bought his cabin. They are the U.S. Geological Survey topographic maps and are a good thing to own in these wild mountains.

"She can't be going far," I say as we step up on a large doorstep of rock and into the cabin. "She has a pig."

"A pig?" he asks incredulously. Bando dislikes pigs as much as I do. A bunch of them from the farm below him got loose this spring and made a mud hole of his garden.

Zella comes in through the back door.

"Did I hear you say Alice ran away?"

"Good morning, Zella," I say. "She sure did. She left me a note saying she was leaving, but she didn't say where she was going or how long she'd be staying."

Zella looks nice this morning in a dark blue jacket and skirt. I guess she's going to work. Her black hair is pulled back from her face with silver combs. Dark-rimmed glasses over her long-lashed eyes make her look very professional and also pretty.

"So, at last she's done it," Zella says with a whimsical smile.

"Done what?" I ask.

"Gone off on her own. She's wanted to do it for a long time."

"She has? She never told me about it."

"Perhaps she didn't want anyone to know where she's gone." She winks at me. I didn't want anyone to know where I was either for fear they'd take me home.

"I think she does want me to know," I say. "She left me a message in the sand along the swamp stream.

She told me she's going east by northeast—to somewhere."

Bando has spread several of the topographical maps
on his big oak table. The maps, which you order
through the United States Department of Interior, U.S.
Geological Survey, are masterpieces of mapmaking.
They reflect the shape of the Earth's surface, portrayed
by contour lines twenty feet apart. These brown lines
are the distinctive characteristic of topographic maps.
They tell you exactly where and how high you are, so
you can never get lost. They also show roads, buildings,
railroads, transmission lines, mines and caves, vegeta-
tion, and towns, cities, rivers, lakes, canals, marshes,
and waterfalls.

Bando leans over the state map.

"You say she's going east by northeast?" he says taking out a compass with a housing that has 360 degrees
marked on it, as well as a clear plastic base-plate with
straight sides that can be used as a ruler. It also has a
directional, or pointer, arrow drawn on it. The compass
is for orienteering—finding your way with a map—and
saves you a lot of time plotting your course. You don't
have to use a protractor to figure out the degrees.

Bando lines up the state map with north and, placing
his compass approximately on the swamp creek, turns
the housing to 70 degrees, or east by northeast.

The directional arrow points to the Helderberg
Mountains.

"Do you suppose she's going there?" I ask.

"That's the most interesting spot on the east by northeast line," Bando says. "Beyond that's Albany, and we know she's not going there.

"But why the Helderbergs?" he muses. "They're not as spectacular as the Catskills or Adirondacks."

"I wouldn't mind going there myself," I say. "Miss Turner said there is a pair of goshawks that nest on the Helderberg Escarpment. I'd sure like to see them."

"Goshawks?" says Bando. "I would, too. I read a book about one. What a remarkable, spirited bird."

"They're the most aggressive of all the birds of prey," I say. "Many of the kings of medieval England preferred them to peregrine falcons—they can capture huge cranes and buzzards. And they're downright ferocious when it comes to defending their young. Miss Turner said the Helderberg pair knocked a man out of their nest tree."

"Let me look at the map of the Helderbergs," Zella says, then picks up the magnifying glass and studies the map Bando spreads out for her.

"I see a lot of waterfalls," she says. On the maps, waterfalls are the blue lines going through brown contour lines drawn closely together, thereby indicating a steep incline or cliff.

"Once Alice told me," Zella goes on, "that her dream was to go on a long hike, clamber beautiful waterfalls, with the water splashing around her, and sleep beside them at night."

"Hey, Bando," I say. "That could be what she's

doing all right. She really does like waterfalls. Remember I told you about the note she left me saying, 'thinking waterfalls'?"

"Yes, I do," Bando says. "But she can't climb waterfalls."

"Why not?" Zella asks.

"Because she's got a pig."

"She's got a pig named Crystal," I explain to Zella.

"How smart of her," Zella says, straightening up from the map. "Pigs are very intelligent. She'll be good company for Alice."

Zella doesn't know much about country life, but she's nice.

"Even an intelligent pig would not be much good on a long hike," I say. "They're no good at all as far as I'm concerned."

"What's wrong with them?" Zella asks.

"You ought to know," Bando says. "They tore up our garden and ate all the carrots and lettuce."

"They root in the ground," I say and wax into a lecture. "They destroy the ground cover so that the birds and animals of the ferns and mosses have no home. I would never let one on my mountain—never."

"That's exactly why I think a pig would be of help to Alice. The pig—what did you say her name was?"

"Crystal."

"Crystal"—she smiles and her eyes shine—"would dig up tubers and bulbs for Alice to eat."

Bando and I look at each other. Zella is right. A pig

would be helpful to Alice. My thinking is taking a different course now. "Pigs are excellent water diviners, too. I recall reading that somewhere. She could help Alice find waterfalls."

"How?" Bando asks, as if I've lost my mind. "How would a pig know Alice *wanted* her to find waterfalls?"

"She talks to that pig," I answer, looking Bando right straight in the eye. I want him to believe this. Animals communicate with each other, and when you learn their language, you can communicate with them too. Scientists as well as animal lovers do this. Bando looks doubtful, so I try to explain.

"It's like I talk to Frightful with love squeaks and whistles and Mrs. Strawberry talks to Slats by blowing air through her lips."

As I speak of Frightful, I realize that I've been so preoccupied with Alice's adventure that I haven't thought about her for hours and hours.

"Now, then," says Bando, turning back to the map. "Let's sum this up. We know where Alice is going in general—east northeast toward the Helderbergs, and she's going via waterfalls."

"Right," I agree.

"So," Bando goes on, "now all we have to do is figure out her route."

"This much I know. She is starting out by going southeast for a short distance," I say.

He takes out the Delhi quadrangle map, the one with our homes on it. The quadrangle maps, which are liter-

ally quadrangles, 16¾ by 22¾ inches, are not like the
county maps. These are land not political boundaries.
Their scale is three and three-quarter inches to the
mile—a lot of space to put down the details. On the
Delhi quadrangle map is Bando's cabin, my mountain,
Mrs. Strawberry's house and farm, as well as all the
buildings in Delhi. My millhouse and tree are not on it,
for which I am grateful. I like privacy.

Bando puts the directional arrow of his compass on
the swamp creek and pencils a line across the page at
157 degrees, south southeast, the second direction Alice
gave us and the first one she took. It intersects Peaks
Brook.

"Of course," I say. "That makes sense. She and the
pig can walk down the streambed quite comfortably.
The water's low. When they get to the West Branch of
the Delaware River, Alice can launch out on her east-
northeast direction to the nearest waterfall."

"Right," Bando says, straightening up and rubbing
his back. "Now, to find her."

"No," I protest. "We don't do that. I feel strongly
about not following her. She wants to do this by herself,
and I think she has every right to."

Bando is shaking his head no.

"When you found me in my tree," I remind him.
"You thought I had every right to be there. You didn't
report me."

"But I kept an eye on you, didn't I?"

"Well, I suppose so—sort of."

"I *did* keep an eye on you, and I think we should keep an eye on Alice."

"What do you think, Zella?" I ask.

"Alice is just fine," she replies. "Why don't you two just let her do her thing."

"Zella, love," says Bando. "You know Alice as well as Sam and I do. She's going to get herself in trouble, bite a chicken thief, siphon milk from a farmer's milk can—remember how she put that tube into my cup of hot chocolate and siphoned all my drink into her cup on the floor?" He chuckles. "I didn't mind—but strangers are not so tolerant."

"She'll be just fine," Zella repeats. "And you *did* mind."

Zella slips her arm in Bando's, and he laughs at himself. I don't even smile because I know only too well that Bando is right. Alice has a knack for getting into scrapes.

"Bando," I say. "I agree. I'm going to follow her. I'll keep out of her sight and I won't stop her. But I want to make sure she doesn't yell 'kidnapper' or siphon milk from a farmer's milk can."

"I'll come with you," he says. "Zella is leaving for a trial that's coming up in Poughkeepsie."

"For goodness' sake," Zella says. "Can't that little girl do something on her own? You two just want an excuse to go hiking."

"That's not so," protests Bando unconvincingly.

Zella smiles at him and picks up her suitcase. She

pauses as she walks toward the door and turns to me.

"Sam, I'm so sorry about Frightful. I thought it might happen eventually, but I hoped that those officials who knew you and your way of life would let you keep her."

I look at the floor so she can't see my misty eyes.

"Leon Longbridge is a fine man," she goes on. "We both know him. I worked with him on a legal case and came to admire him. He'll see to it that Frightful is given good care."

I'm really glad to hear that Zella likes Leon Longbridge, because I don't. But her words make me feel a lot better.

Zella gives Bando a hug and a kiss and leaves. We hear the engine of the four-wheel drive start up and listen until it is out of hearing.

"Let's begin where Alice drew her compass in the sand," Bando says as he takes down his packbasket from the wall. In it he puts a bedroll, cup, spoon, some raisins, a collapsible fishing rod and a change of clothes, a raincoat, and a couple of cans of stew. The topographic maps are folded and put in a waterproof holder, then placed in a pocket of the fishing jacket he's wearing.

"I'm ready," he says. "Shall I wait here until you get your equipment?"

"I'm ready," I answer pointing to my belt pack stuffed with the venison and nuts I put there this morning. Then I pat my pockets where I keep fishing lines and my flint and steel, and bring out my sling, now strung with rawhide. "I never leave my mountain without food and gear for a week," I say.

"How far do you think Alice has gotten?" Bando asks.

"Not far," I answer. "She left the mountain three days ago, but she couldn't have made a sun compass the day after Frightful was confiscated because of the haze in the valley. There were no shadows all that day, I recall. I think she started off the next day when the sun was bright. She can't be more than ten or fifteen miles from here with that pig. We can do that in half a day."

Bando checks around the cabin before we leave. Zella has made it cozy with two rocking chairs, a patchwork quilt on the bed, colorful posters, and bright copper pots at the fireplace. I look down at the wood floor.

"You did a nice job here," I say.

"I saved my marriage, that's what I did," he answers and winks at me.

As we walk across Bando's meadow, he whistles; I throw back my head, and, feeling free as the wind, breathe in the fresh mountain air. Although I am heavy-hearted, my spirits are rising. To walk in nature is always good medicine.

Entering the woods, we take a deer trail to the bottom of the mountain, then cut over to Mrs. Strawberry's field. We stop at the sand spit and Alice's sun compass.

The bobolinks are singing in the fields, two herons are flying toward their roost, and grasshoppers are stridulating at our feet.

"Good old Alice," I say to Bando now that I know we are going to find her very soon. "I might have stuck myself on the mountaintop working hard all summer if it hadn't been for her."

IN WHICH

I Learn to Think Like a Pig

Bando stands over the sun compass squinting, scratching his head, and finally grinning as he compares it with his own compass.

"The crazy thing's quite accurate," he says and takes out the quadrangle map of Delhi. Spreading it on the sand, he gets down on his hands and knees and studies it. "Sam, we're going to have to think like Alice to find her. Look here. If you were Alice, where would you go after you got to Peaks Brook?"

I get down beside him and imagine I am Alice as I read the map.

"If I were her," I say, "when I got to the West Branch of the Delaware, I'd follow it to the most powerful stream coming off the highest mountain and go up it to a waterfall."

"Good. That's what I'd do if I were Alice. We're off!"

Walking into the sun, now a hand span over the trees, we follow the slow stream to Peaks Brook. This brook, which starts on the east side of my mountain, is vigorous and so cold it feels as if it were melted snow. I avoid wading in it and stick to its stony edge.

Since it's only two miles to the West Branch, and maybe fifteen miles to Alice, we go slowly, stopping to admire a handsome, almost pure white sycamore and an enormous eastern cottonwood as big or bigger than my tree. Bando lingers over a rock outcrop, and we are happy to see a swatch of rare bluebells. It is a hot day and the icy stream cools the air.

As we go, the brook plays pranks. Here and there it cuts through rocks, leaving no shores to walk on, and we are forced to jump downstream from boulder to boulder. In high spirits, we whoop as we leap. It's wonderful to be out on the trail.

As we zag along, I practice with my sling, missing eighteen times out of twenty. Not good, but not bad. A wolf pack misses its prey sixteen out of twenty tries.

Finally, we go under the highway and railroad bridge and come out on the flats of the West Branch of the Delaware.

"Now, we've got another problem," Bando says, looking around. "Did she go downstream or upstream?

"She's going east northeast now," I say. "Where does that send her?"

"Upstream," he says after taking a sighting with his compass.

Bando puts the map away and starts off.

"Let's not go yet," I say. "The fishing looks good here. I'll get us some lunch."

I catch three pumpkinseed sunfish and a catfish while Bando gathers tender dandelion leaves, chicory greens, and wild carrots for salad. At the same time, he looks for pig tracks.

"No tracks," he reports. "I hope we are thinking like Alice." He takes a seat on a rock and watches me make a fire with my flint and steel.

"Maybe," he muses, "there are no tracks because Crystal's a little pig and Alice is carrying her."

"I doubt it," I reply. "Alice has been talking to this pig for months, and she wasn't a piglet when they met. Maybe we're just not on their course."

I steam the fish and vegetables in violet leaves, and we eat by the river, admiring the kingfishers who dive into the water and come up with fish every time. Then we push on.

Farther along we come to the confluence of the Little Delaware and the West Branch, and Bando takes out his compass and map again.

"The West Branch will take us right through Delhi. Would you want to go through Delhi with a pig on a leash if you were Alice?"

"No."

"Look at the map, then," he says. "We have a problem ahead."

I see what he means. If we take the Little Delaware

and avoid Delhi, we will be way off course. The only other choice, as far as I can see, is to climb Federal Hill and it's nine hundred feet almost straight up.

"That's awfully steep for a pig," I say, "but I'm no expert on pigs."

"As a matter of fact," Bando says. "It may not be too steep. I read a well-researched book about three pigs who followed cattle drovers across prairies and over mountains on a trek to Montana."

That's Bando for you. He always gets his knowledge from reading.

Nevertheless, before making up my mind to climb Federal Hill, I tell Bando to stand still and I spiral out from him in a wider and wider sweep until I have covered almost the entire delta of the Little Delaware and the West Branch.

"Bando!" I shout.

"What?"

"Pig tracks."

He joins me at a trot.

"Pig tracks?" he asks dubiously as he looks at the cloven prints. "They look like deer to me."

"No. Deer prints are much more pointed and tapered. These are quite rounded."

Bando nods and puts his hand beside the prints. "We can certainly say that Crystal is no baby piglet. Those prints are as big as my palm," he observes, and we start off again.

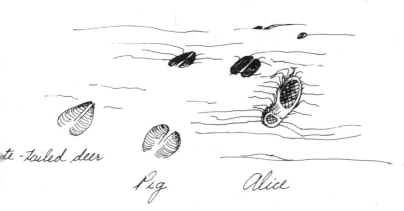

te -tailed deer

Pig   Alice

The tracks lead us through a shallows in the river to the other side, then east by northeast to the bottom of Federal Hill. Near the far edge of the flood plain I find Alice's footsteps in a stretch of muddy sand.

"Hello, little sister," I hoot in excitement. "There you are!"

Grinning with satisfaction, I follow her tracks into the woods where they soon disappear on the leafy trail. But Crystal's do not, and Bando and I follow her up the steep mountain. Then, almost at the top, her tracks disappear.

"The pig took off like a bird," Bando says, studying the last footprint. I spiral again, moving out from that print as I search for another. When I am almost ready to give up, I come upon a trampled and routed garden of May apples.

"I've found her," I call. "She stopped for lunch."

"Let's take five," says Bando and sits down. "That's a steep climb and, besides, we're making good time.

They can't be too far ahead. That pig is hardly a grey-hound."

The sunlight filters through lacy hemlock needles and we stretch out on our backs, chewing the tasty twigs of a spicebush and silently admiring the forest.

"You know, Sam," Bando finally says. "I remember something else about pigs from that book."

"Really? What?"

"They bite. They can be as mean and dangerous as a guard dog. They even kill and eat snakes."

"Is that right? I'm glad to hear that." Although Alice is very good at taking care of herself, I'm happy to know pigs can bite. I smile and look at Bando. "I'm beginning to like that pig," I say.

"So am I."

Bando chuckles.

"What's so funny?"

"I'd sure hate to be the one who tries to tackle Alice and her pig."

"So would I," I say, shaking my head. "They both bite."

I spread out the Delhi quadrangle map.

"I figure Alice was sitting right here where we are two days ago," I say. "And at about this time of day. If so, and if I were her, I'd be looking for a waterfall and a campsite right now."

Bando glances at the sun and nods. I take out the map.

"Fitches Brook is it," I say, pointing to a cluster of

brown contour lines drawn close together which indicate a steep hill. There is a blue line through them. Together they say "waterfall."

"It's the only stream with a slope steep enough to make a waterfall and close enough to be reached before evening." I point to a submerged swamp symbol. "The brook begins here." I measure. "We have about four miles to go."

"Let's get along, then," Bando says, rising to his feet. "We'll want to have enough light when we get there to do a little fishing."

It is easy to follow dear old Crystal, as we are now calling her, and at about 4:00 P.M. we arrive at a reed-filled mountain swamp in a dark spruce forest where Fitches Brook starts.

Bando unfolds his collapsible fishing rod, and I gather cattail tubers and catch a mess of frogs for dinner. It's still too early to stop for the night, so we fish and gather May apples for dessert as we follow the splashing stream downhill.

I almost missed Alice's camp. It wasn't by the steepest waterfall, as I thought it would be, but considerably below and under, of all things, a dead oak. I passed that tree with only a quick glance, because it didn't look like anything Alice would pick, and then something occurred to me. I turned back. The leaves and sticks under the tree had been recently placed there. They did not match the colors of the leaves and sticks around them because their wet dark bottoms were up, not down.

Alice and I always cover our campsite with leaves when we depart so that no one will know we have been there. Those displaced leaves have a distinctive look to the knowing eye—jumbled and unnatural.

I kick a few aside, looking for blackened fireplace rocks or wood that would tell me Alice had camped here. Finding none where the strewn leaves are, I search the other side of the oak.

I come upon holes in the ground that could have been made by none other than a pig. They are outlined by rounded hoof prints and have sniff marks in them. Ha, I say to myself.

"Bando," I call. "A pig has been here."

Bando joins me, folding his rod as he contemplates the dead tree and the leaf-strewn ground.

"Alice slept here?" he asks incredulously.

"She did." I pick up a recently fire-blackened stone.

"If she loves beautiful waterfalls so much," he says, "why this unattractive place?"

"It's not unattractive to the pig," I answer. "We're not only going to have to think like Alice, but also like a pig."

"Got it," he says and picks up a half-eaten black-snake. "Pig kill," he says. "It's been thrashed and bitten. The book says that's how pigs kill snakes." He looks around, then points to another snake, soaking up the last sun of the day on a limb of the dead tree. "We're in blacksnake habitat. Another reason for Alice and her pig to stop here."

"Bando," I say, "Pigs are omnivores. We've got to think snakes, fungi, grasshoppers, and big juicy moths as well as bulbs and roots." He sighs. I go on. "Here we are among fungi and snakes. It's clear Crystal is making decisions for Alice."

"And us," he mumbles, taking out his bedroll and spreading it under the leafless tree. I gather pine boughs for my bed, cook the frogs legs and cattail tubers, then put out the fire.

After eating we stretch out on the ground. Gradually the sky darkens and fireflies flash their love lights as the males rise through the trees by the brook.

"Bando?"

"Yes?"

"We're doing fine. I think we'll find Alice tomorrow."

"Maybe," he answers. "Trouble is, she knows where she's going. We don't."

"That's true," I reply resignedly.

A screech owl calls from the dead oak, and I look up. There is nothing so magical as a tree with an owl in it. The dead oak has come to life.

The little owl brings Frightful back to mind.

"Bando?"

"Yes, Sam."

"Do you think it's too late in the season for Frightful to breed? We're way into June."

"It probably is, but the geneticists do amazing things today."

Owl tree

I'm glad to hear that, but I still can't go to sleep.
"Bando?"
"Yes?"
"Have you seen the place where they keep the falcons at the university—the peregrine mew?"
"Yes. I have a friend on the staff there. You got me interested in peregrine falcons, and he got me interested in the effort to keep them on the planet with us."
"Tell me about the mew."
"Well, it's an enormous barn that is divided into apartments for paired falcons. Each mew has a high wooden shelf that resembles a cliff where the birds nest in the wilds. The females lay their eggs on these platforms. Some pairs will mate in captivity, others like Frightful, who is imprinted on you, must be artificially inseminated. Once the eggs are laid, the birds incubate them, and when they hatch, the sight of the nestlings triggers a ferocious parental love. The parents tend their young until they fly.

"It's a nice place, Sam, not like a cliff above a wild river, but nice. You'd like it."

I close my eyes and see Frightful incubating her eggs. A hot wind rises out of the valley, rustling the leaves and making me sleepy at last.

IN WHICH

Bando Finds Some Old Adirondack Furniture

At dawn we return our campsite pretty much to its original pristine appearance and walk on down the brook.

Shortly we are out of the forest and standing in a field. A large farm lies in the valley below.

"We've lost Alice's trail somewhere," I say. "If I were her, I would not go down through a farm with a pig on a leash."

"I would," Bando says. "There's a corncrib down there. Pigs like corn, you know."

We look at each other as the same thought strikes us. Alice has already been to the farm. About a hundred yards back we had noticed several corncobs along the shore of Fitches Brook. Still unaccustomed to thinking like a pig, we had agreed that raccoons had been at work on some farmer's crop.

Back we go, avalanching rocks as we scramble up the

shaley streambed and arrive at the embankment where we had seen an ear of corn. It's gone. I am searching upstream for it and any others when Bando calls. He is pointing to the stream bank. Four corncobs have been laid there in the shape of an arrow. Alice has been here. They point to a big flat rock where a squirrel is now stuffing kernels from another ear of corn in his cheeks. You can't leave anything sitting around in the woods or someone will get it. Even hard deer antlers are eaten by white-footed deer mice.

I leap across the stream on the rocks, the squirrel runs, and I pick up his ear of corn. There are broad teeth marks on it which are not squirrel. Could be deer, but it's not. It's pig. Pig droppings nearby clinch the identification, and then, looking around, I see Crystal's tracks in the soft loam. I'm off.

"Not so fast," Bando calls. "Come back. I've found something else."

On bare earth in the sun is another compass. This one is different from the first. Alice has propped up a stick at a 45-degree angle to the ground. On it hangs a stone on a string. Under it is a north-south directional stick. Smiling, I recall how Alice and I made a compass like this last spring. We placed a marker on the shadow that the hanging rock cast in the morning. Then, when the sun passed the meridian, we put another marker on the afternoon stone-shadow. Between the two marks and directly under the suspended rock, we laid a stick. We had a north-south line.

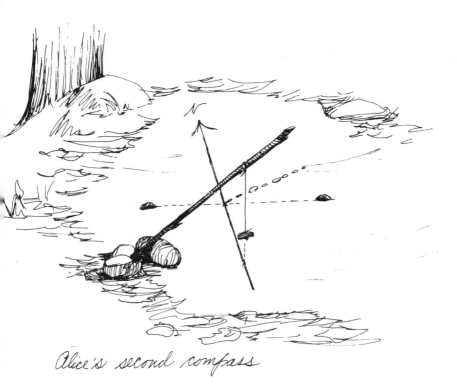

Alice's second compass

"She's checking her direction," I say.

"Well, she's got north, all right," Bando says, looking at his compass. "Her stick points to within 3 degrees of true north."

"And she plotted her directional line too," I say, pointing to the little pebbles lined up there.

"Ah, ha!" Bando lays his compass with the directional arrow lined up with the pebbles. Carefully he turns the compass housing until the arrow and north are lined up. He looks at the bearing marker. "She's going more easterly now—80 degrees."

We spread the county map on the ground and lay a grass blade from our stream location across the page at

80 degrees. The blade crosses the Schoharie Reservoir and intercepts Manorkill Falls.

I count contour lines and multiply by twenty. "Wow," I say. "That waterfall drops almost straight down a hundred feet."

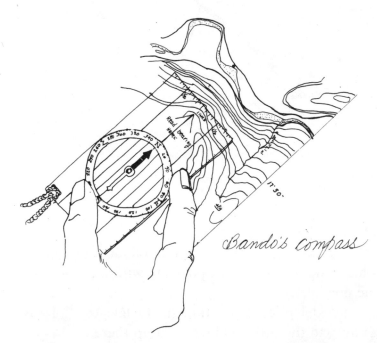

Bando's compass

"Manorkill Falls," Bando says. "I've read it's spectacular. If I were a girl who loved waterfalls, I'd be headed right for it."

"In fact," I say. "I'm so sure she's going there that we should go directly to it without losing any more time following pig tracks."

"Good idea," Bando agrees.

There are no trails or roads up here, so, by lining up trees to keep us going in a straight line, and by reading the quadrangle maps to avoid cliffs and marshes, we strike off across the top of the mountain range.

We traverse fields and forests, walk through barren lands where quails and woodcocks fly up at our feet, and, after twelve miles of bushwhacking, enter the Plattekill State Forest. We are greeted by a flock of wild turkeys, big, noisy, and glorious. They gobble and fly off, miraculously missing limbs and trunks as they zip through the forest. I could never hit one of those with my sling.

Although we're tired, the top of the mountain we're climbing calls to us, and we scramble on to its summit. Here we can see the Catskill, Helderberg, and distant Adirondack Mountains. I understand why people climb mountains. I am an eagle.

Bando sits down. We've been walking hard since 6:00 A.M., almost ten hours, and we're both glad to rest. The trek was rough because we stayed in the forests, where the understory is a jungle of hazelnut, viburnum, and twisted young hardwoods fighting for the sun. Travelling through them was work.

I offer Bando some smoked venison and dried apples. He eats heartily.

"I'm ready to stop for the night," he says. "I don't think we have to hurry now. If I were Alice and had reached Manorkill Falls, I'd stay for at least a day or two, wouldn't you?"

"I sure would," I say, noting the scratches on his arms and the smudges of dirt on his cheeks. "You're right, we don't have to hurry."

While he makes his bed, I practice with my sling. On the trek today, I missed nineteen out of twenty targets. I'm not doing so well. I guess it takes a lot of practice.

Later, Bando sleeps. I watch the stars and think of Frightful.

I wake early, pick a few Labrador tea leaves and brew them in Bando's tin cup. Then I gather a batch of day-lily buds for our breakfast. These I moisten in dew and dip in hazelnuts I pounded to a powder with a stone. I steam them in spicebush leaves.

With a catbird diving at us to chase us away from his nest, we leave the mountaintop on a northeasterly course. Bando is a little stiff and sore this morning, so we walk slowly, enjoying the vistas from the skyline of this mountain range.

We stop frequently to consult the map, whether we need to or not. Map reading gives us a good excuse to rest.

"Sam, look here," Bando says during one of these stops. "There's a power line below us. It leads to the road at the bottom of Manorkill Falls. It'll be a lot easier to walk on the cleared land under those wires than in this dense forest. Shall we take it?"

I agree we should, and within a few miles we break out of the tangled undergrowth into a meadow under the power line. We walk in daylilies, Queen Anne's lace, and the last daisies of June. A few black-eyed Susans bloom to say midsummer is nearly here.

We make good time, and I practice with my sling on the steel tower struts. There are so many that if I don't hit the one I aim at, I hit the one next to it. This is very satisfying, for although I'm not hitting my target, I am hitting something.

As we follow the meadow down the last steep slope of the mountain range, I see a patch of evening primroses near a stone fence. The roots of this flower are very good if you boil them long enough to remove the peppery taste. Taking my hunting knife from its sheath on my belt, I kneel down to dig but whoop instead.

"Bando! Crystal's been here!"

He runs down the hillside. "By golly, she has!"

"We stopped thinking pig," I say. "Crystal must have led Alice to the power lines. All kinds of edible plants grow in this habitat." I point to an uprooted primrose. "Including one of my favorites. Crystal has good taste." Getting to my feet, I glance around. She has also dug up a batch of Jerusalem artichokes, and I pick up one of the potatolike tubers she missed.

"Thank you, Crystal," I say and stuff it in my pouch along with the primrose.

"How do you think Crystal found all of this food?" Bando asks after we have started off again. "And I presume she did find it, not Alice."

"Smelled it, I guess," I say. "We humans will never know how meadows or mountains smell, but deer and

Jerusalem artichoke

horses and pigs do." Bando sniffs deeply and shakes his head.

"We were left out when it comes to smelling things," he says. "I would love to be able to smell a mountain and follow my nose to it."

Crystal's tracks are quite obvious now that we know she has been here, and we are able to trot along as we follow her down the steep slope. Bando veers off to the left and stops.

"Looks like a struggle here," he says pointing to tracks that are dug in deep, as if Crystal were resisting being pulled somewhere.

"Seems Alice is dragging her into those woods," Bando says.

"I wonder why," I ask, trying to think like Alice. I look for an answer in the mountains and rolling terrain but find none.

On we go, following the pig tracks. Presently we enter

a dark woods of very old yellow birches and again lose Crystal. The forest ends, and we are on a steep hillside looking across a valley at the famous profile of White Man Mountain.

"Bando!" I say. "I know what Alice is up to. The summer house of John Burroughs, the nature writer, is somewhere around here. I read parts of his books to Alice last winter. That's the mountain he loved. An artist sketched it for one of his books."

We wind down and around and within a quarter of a mile come upon John Burroughs' grave. It is surrounded by a stone wall and covered with lilies of the valley.

Bando finds some shelled beechnuts and hazelnuts lying at the base of a hollow tree near the grave.

"Could this be Alice?" he asks, bringing the nuts to me. "I'm suspicious of everything now."

I look at the nuts all neatly peeled and recognize the handiwork of a white-footed deer mouse. I put my hand in the hollow and find more.

"Alice has been here," I say. "But she did not shell the nuts. She raided a deer-mouse pantry. Deer mice take the coats off the seeds and nuts before they store them. You're real lucky when you find one. It's like opening a can of cocktail nuts. They're ready to eat." I pop a hazelnut in my mouth.

We take to a country road, where posters advertising the Roxbury Country Fair are nailed to every telephone pole.

"I love fairs," says Bando. "Think we have time to go?"

"No," I answer. "I don't think Alice is going to stay at Manorkill Falls as long as you think she is. There are lots of beautiful cascades in the Helderbergs."

We walk on in silence, round a bend and stop.

"There it is," I exclaim, pointing to a small brown house. "That's Woodchuck Lodge, John Burroughs' summer home."

"It is?" says Bando. "Well, as far as I'm concerned, it's the capital of Adirondack furniture. Look at that house!" Bando takes off his packbasket and gets out a notebook and pencil.

Woodchuck Lodge is small and rustic, with a sharply gabled roof and a porch railing of twisted limbs and branches. The porch furniture looks like my lounging chair, and the trim on the gable is a weaving of gnarled oaks and maple branches.

"Woodchuck Lodge," I read on the door, "is a National Monument supervised by the National Park Service." At this moment no one is here but us.

I start a small fire in the outdoor fireplace, wrap the primrose and artichoke in maple leaves, and clip some young shoots of a pokeweed.

"You know, Sam," Bando says as he sketches and watches me concoct a wild, savory lunch, "I think I'll just open one of the cans of stew."

As I put his food on the fire, I see four stones to my left and recognize a pathfinder's sign. Three stones are stacked one on top of the other, the fourth, on the ground beside them, points the direction the person is taking.

"Bando," I say, squatting beside the sign, "Alice has been here. She's changing course, going in the direction of that stone on the ground."

"How do you know it's Alice?" Bando asks.

"Pig tracks right here and an acorn, her woodland signature."

Bando lays his compass beside the directional stone and adjusts it.

"Seventy degrees," he says. "She's going east by northeast again."

"She's off to Manorkill Falls," I say and remove the hot stew from the fire.

IN WHICH
I Become Royalty

Alice is not at Manorkill Falls. I was certain she would be.

Bando and I climbed the steep gorge to the top, searching every cave and ledge along the ascent, and found no sign of her or her pig, no clues to say that they were here.

"If Alice," Bando says as we stand on the rim of the

gorge, "was in search of a beautiful waterfall, she should be right here where I am." The water roars and tumbles below us, sending up a soft spray that nurtures mosses and maidenhair ferns where it falls.

"But she's not," I say. "And I don't think she will be."

"Why?" he asks.

"Pigs don't care about views and water music. No sensible pig, and Crystal is a sensible pig as we well know, is going to let anyone, not even Alice, lead her up to this place. Federal Hill is one thing, but Crystal would need pitons for this ascent," I say, looking at all the watercress available for dinner.

"That's right. But where is she then?" Bando asks, not really expecting me to answer. Rather, he looks for an answer himself by taking out the map of Schoharie county, which we're in, and the map of Albany county, which we're coming to, and spreading them contiguously. As for me, I've given up trying to think like Alice for the day, and turn to a job I know I can do.

I dig a beetle larva out of a decaying log and put it on a thornbush fishhook I made and tied to a fine cord of deer tendon. Then, taking off my moccasins, I wade into the cold water and cast into a pool below a submerged log. A dragonfly skims over the surface, his crystal wings reflecting the sunlight.

Wop! I yank, and hook a large trout. Playing it carefully so it won't break my line as it darts from side to side, I concentrate on dinner. After a lively battle, I land the fish.

Bando is still bent over the maps. I clean the trout and wrap it in May-apple leaves, then dig a hole in the earth and build a fire. When the coals are hot, I push them into the hole, place the fish on them, and cover all with leaves, then soil.

"There's a farm at the bottom of the gorge," Bando says as I brush the dirt off my hands and sit down beside him. "There aren't many around. The land's too steep."

"Hmmm," I say, trying to think like my sister. "Let's go there and ask the farmer if she's been by for corn."

"Let's not ask people and get them all stirred up. We know she's all right, but they won't. They'll call the police and we don't want that."

"I'm going to ask, anyway," I say. "I think those stones at John Burroughs' home meant change of plans as well as change of direction."

"Why do you think that?"

"Because that's the first time she's used a plain old pathfinder's sign. She wanted to be sure that message was seen. Furthermore, she signed it with an acorn so I'd make no mistake about who laid the stones.

"And," I go on, still trying to think like Alice, "I've got a hunch she's left the change of plans with a person. Once we talked about how we might leave clues with people if we ever got off the mountain. It's like her to try it, so I'm going to take a chance and speak to that farmer. He's the only one around for miles, and since she's not at this falls, she's doing something radically different."

"I still don't think you should," Bando says as I serve him the fish on a nice thin slab of slate, garnished with watercress and crisp daylily roots. "But maybe you're right."

We find a log and sit down. A woodthrush sings. His song sounds like water spilling down the rocks in a cool, dark forest. As I listen, I thank Alice in spite of myself. Were it not for her, I would not be hearing that glorious song on top of this magnificent gorge.

Bando eats and goes back to the maps.

"Look at this, Sam," he says brightly. He is feeling better with sweet trout in his belly. "There's got to be some granddaddy of a waterfall at the Helderberg Escarpment. A large stream runs right off the edge of that eight-hundred-foot cliff." I get down on my knees and look.

"Wow!" I say. "I'll bet Alice is going there." I study the map. "And there are fields and farms nearby for Crystal. I think we're on Alice's brain wave now."

"Let's go," Bando says. "I'd like to see the goshawks." He packs his belongings, and we start the long descent to the bottom of the gorge.

About an hour later we are standing in the enormous rock bowl that holds the reservoir. The sun has just gone down.

"Where's the farm?" I ask.

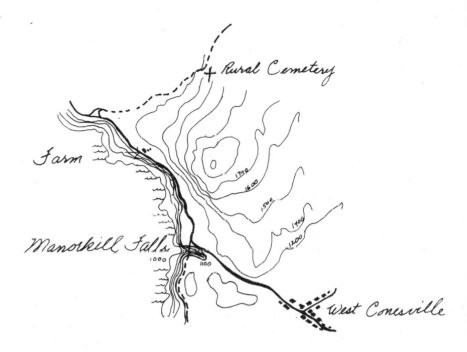

"Up the road about half a mile on the right." I start off.

"Hold on," Bando says. "I really don't like this idea, so I'll let you go alone to ask about Alice."

"You're not coming?"

"I'll meet you later. Zella asked me to give her a call if I got the chance." He shifts his packbasket. "West Conesville is about half a mile from here. Since it'll soon be dark and we can't go on, this looks like a good time to telephone her."

"All right," I say reluctantly. "Where shall we meet?"

"I saw a rural cemetery on the map about a mile beyond the farm. Make camp and I'll meet you there."

"When?"

"I'm not sure. Don't wait up for me."

As I approach the farm, I slow down to study the situation I'm walking into. The land is well tended, the buildings strong and freshly painted. This is reassuring, because these things speak of a hardworking farmer, and hardworking farmers are usually sincere people. The ones I know have no time for pretense. They answer yes or no. I trust this farmer will do likewise when I ask if he's seen Alice.

The farmhouse is very old. It has two small low windows on the second floor, and the clapboard is slightly wider than the boards on houses today. I glance at the corncrib as I pass it and hope that Alice did not help herself to a meal for Crystal. I scold myself for thinking this.

I tuck my shirt in my jeans and, combing my hair with a teasel-weed head I found near the corncrib, I walk up the steps to the house.

As I lift the knocker, I read the Dutch name, Van Sandtford, beneath it. The Dutch were the first settlers in this part of New York, so it could be that this is a pioneer family. Thinking this helps me relax. I understand pioneers. I am one with them.

Footsteps resound and the door is opened by a large, bony gentleman. He has sandy hair, a long nose, and deep-set blue eyes. He looks like one of the portraits of the pioneers on the walls of the Delhi library.

"Sir," I begin. "I'm inquiring about my sister. She

was purchasing corn. Did she by any chance come by here today?"

"Alice, you mean? The pretty girl with the pig?" My heart bangs; I'm on the track.

"Yes, Alice," I say and smile broadly, wondering what to say next. I am saved by Mr. Van Sandtford.

"She stayed here for a few days with her pig," he says. "But she's gone on to the Livingstonville fair with my daughter, Hanni."

"Oh," I say, trying not to cry out in disappointment.

"She and Hanni met at the Roxbury fair, and Hanni invited her to stay here until the 4-H Club fair at Livingstonville started."

So that's why she gave me the change-of-plans sign at John Burroughs' place, I say to myself. She saw the Roxbury fair posters and went down to see it. She wasn't at Manorkill Falls because she got a ride.

"My son, Hendrik," Mr. Van Sandtford goes on, "drove Alice and Hanni to Livingstonville last evening with their hogs. Hanni raises hogs, too. The girls are going to sleep in the barn with their animals." I must look surprised, for he says, "I hope that's all right, and that your family won't object."

"No, no. It's fine," I say.

Mr. Van Sandtford steps out on the porch to join me, and his eyes sweep over his farm as he checks barn, silo, and fields in the manner of a farmer. A cow might be sick or a fox might be in the chicken coop. Apparently all is well. He sits on the railing.

"I love the way these 4-H Club kids take care of their animals," he goes on. "You'd think they were their children."

I walk down the steps, trying to make an exit.

"I hope Alice hasn't been a burden," I say.

"A burden? Alice?" he replies. "She worked very hard. She cleaned the hog barn, swept the porch, and helped Hanni and Hendrick with the cows and horses. She's a great little girl."

"Good," I answer almost too eagerly.

"Clever sow Alice has," her host continues. "Isn't it amazing the way she rolls over?"

"Yes. Yes, it is," I stutter and jump down the stone path, hoping to escape before it becomes evident that I don't know much about Crystal.

Mrs. Van Sandtford has come out on the porch and is looking at me as if she knew something about me that I don't know. I feel uneasy.

"We enjoyed Alice," she says. "I just know she's going to win a blue ribbon with that Spotted Poland China of hers." Spotted Poland China? I am thinking she means dishes, until I realize she is talking about Alice's pig.

"Well, I appreciate your helping her," I repeat awkwardly. "She was so anxious to get to the pig fair that she couldn't wait for me to drive her there." I bite my lips. I am getting myself in trouble. Huck Finn is right—truth is better and actually safer than a lie.

I hurry toward the gate.

"Wouldn't you like a cup of tea before you go, Mr. Van Rensselaer?" Mrs. Van Sandtford asks.

I suck in air. Mr. Van Rensselaer? Now what is Alice up to?

"No, thank you," I say. "I've really got to go." With that empty remark, I smile and leave.

Halfway to the rural cemetery, I think of something, turn around, and run the mile to West Conesville. Bando told me not to wait up for him. I know why.

The full moon is rising over the chimneys and gabled rooftops of the little town as I walk up the steps to the Ruffed Grouse Hotel and enter the lobby. At the registration desk I tap a bell and a tall man appears.

"Sir," I say. "Would you please tell Mr. Zackery that Sam Gribley is here."

"He's in the dining room," he replies and directs me to a large room hung with red drapes and dimly lit with electric sconces.

"Sam!"

"Bando." It's as I suspected. He's eating.

"Sit down, Sam. Have a bite on me."

"I've eaten."

He grins sheepishly.

"Sam, I'm not as young as you are. I just have to get a good meal before I can think like a pig and a girl again."

"Well, you don't have to think like either anymore," I say. "I found Alice and the pig."

"Where?"

"They're at the 4-H Club fair in Livingstonville."

Bando puts down his fork. "A 4-H Club fair? Alice? I wonder what she's up to there?"

He opens the menu to the list of desserts, and I think about my new name but can't make any sense out of it.

"Who are the Van Rensselaers, Bando?" I finally ask.

"The Van Rensselaers? They were the feudal lords of what is now Albany county. Before we were a democracy—in fact, in the 1600s—they were given hundreds of thousands of acres of land by the Dutch king—all of Albany county. They divided this land into 120-acre parcels and rented them to their countrymen who came to the New World. The Van Rensselaers made fortunes and became a powerful and influential family. Why?"

"Meet Sam Van Rensselaer," I say, extending my hand.

"Alice?"

"Alice is calling herself Alice Van Rensselaer, so that makes me Sam Van Rensselaer."

"Well," Bando smiles. "With a name like that you can go to all the fanciest places. The Van Rensselaers were colonial New York's royalty."

This does not help me figure out why she picked that name. She must be trying to tell me something, but what?

Bando finishes his meal, and we leave the dining room, with me dashing ahead for the door.

"Sam," Bando takes my arm. "I've taken a room here."

"Really?"

"I'm tired," he says. "I need a comfortable bed."

He does look tired. I have been very thoughtless.

"I'm sorry," I say. "I didn't know you were *that* exhausted, or I would have stopped earlier."

"One night's good sleep will fix me up," he says, putting his hand on his hip and limping like an old man.

"Sure," I laugh. "Sleep well."

"There are twin beds in my room. You can have one of them. If it's too soft, there's always the floor."

"No, thanks," I say. "I couldn't sleep indoors if I wanted to. I'll meet you in the cemetery at sunup."

"Zella sends her love," he calls as I leave.

Love goes a long way. I stride down the street.

IN WHICH

I Get News of Alice

We leave the Catskills behind north of the cemetery and enter the Helderbergs. I know we are in them when the forest trees change. Maples and hemlocks are replaced by yellow birch and the northland's black spruce. Dark bogs pock the mountaintops. We sink up to our calves in one of these, so avoid the others by checking the map and plotting a course around them.

As we bushwhack along, the mountains themselves

tell me we have arrived. The Helderbergs are made up of layers of limestone and shale, through which underground streams and rivers have carved miles of caverns. Some near the surface have caved in, leaving gaping sink holes in the land. Others are walk-in caves.

These are magnets, and we explore each one we come upon. Deep in them we can hear subterranean rivers rushing off through the netherworld, and our voices echo and reecho through the halls. We see a dimly illumed underground waterfall and climb down to it for a dark thundering shower.

We spend the night by a cavern and before sunup are jogging along toward the 4-H Club fair. I am concerned about Alice's using the name Van Rensselaer. I can sense an Alice-scrape coming up. Imposters are not appreciated, not even yellow-headed ones.

Shortly after sunrise we come down the steep road into Livingstonville, a small town of no more than forty houses and stores cozied at the confluence of the Catskill and Lake creeks.

Virtually no cars pass us; the sidewalks are empty, and the homes, which were built many years ago, stand gray or paint-chipped behind walls of lilacs and groves of stately trees. Modernizing is not fashionable in Livingstonville. Even the store is an old grocery-gas-hardware-feed store and luncheonette–post office that dates back to the twenties, Bando says. It's a wonderful town.

We enter the all-purpose store and sit down at the

luncheonette counter. Only four people are here, which
is the right number for any store as far as I'm concerned. Bando picks up the menu.

"Coffee, homemade sausage sandwich, and straw-
berry-rhubarb pie," he says to the woman behind the
counter. She also seems to be the postmistress, for she
is sorting mail as well as listening to Bando's order.

I stare at him. We've just finished a breakfast of fish
chowder and sow-thistle leaves, and here he is eating
again. No wonder he has a paunch! Or he did have one.
He's walked it off, I see.

"Sam," Bando says. "What do you want to eat?"

"Nothing," I reply. "I'm stuffed."

When Bando's breakfast is set before him, I turn to
the burly man beside me.

"Sir," I say to the stranger, emboldened by the com-
forting shelves of canning jars and bins of nails and feed.
"Can you tell me how to get to the Livingstonville fairgrounds?"

"Fairgrounds?" His voice is so low it vibrates. "Ain't
no fairgrounds in Livingstonville."

"There aren't? But there's supposed to be a 4-H Club
fair in Livingstonville." I'm devastated as Alice slips
away again. We just can't ever quite catch up with her.
The postmistress finishes sorting the mail and brings me
a glass of water.

"I just happened to overhear you," she says, pushing
back her gray hair. "I'll bet you're looking for that hog
show."

"I am," I reply.

"It's at the Monroe Farm, a piece up Hauverville Road toward Rensselaerville."

"Is that what you're looking for?" the man beside me asks. I nod. "Mammie's right. The hog show's up there on that farm. Lots of kids. Nice kids. They like pigs."

I impatiently wait for Bando to finish his meal so I can go outside and talk to him without being overheard. I know why Alice took the name Van Rensselaer. The postmistress unwittingly gave me the answer. I nudge Bando. He picks up the newspaper lying on the counter, sips his coffee, and reads. He's not ready to leave.

I count to one hundred slowly, then watch the postmistress read a postcard before putting it in a box.

"Here's a news story on the 4-H Club fair," Bando says. I count tractor tires. He turns the page and reads on.

"This note in the personal column ought to interest you. 'Skri. Hacking falcons at Huyck Preserve, 6:00 P.M., 25th of June. Check R library for final arrangements.' "

"That *is* interesting," I say, leaning over his shoulder to read this item.

I ask the postmistress where the Huyck Preserve is.

"Just this side of Rensselaerville," she answers, and I thank her and get right to my feet. Bando is still reading, so I look at the jelly jars. My clay ones are nicer.

Finally he lays down the paper, pays his bill, and we leave.

"Bando," I say as soon as we step on the sidewalk. "I know why Alice used the name Van Rensselaer."

"You do? Why?"

"She's telling me her destination."

"You're kidding. Where *is* she going?"

"To Rensselaerville."

"How do you know that?"

"Let me look at the Rensselaerville quadrangle map," I say and open it on the hood of a truck. "Yep, there's a waterfall there. It drops about a hundred feet."

"She sent a message by changing her name?" Bando says incredulously. "That's pretty farfetched. She doesn't even know we're following her."

"She sure does."

"Come on, Sam. She's been at least twenty miles ahead of us ever since we left."

"But she's playing On the Track."

"So?" He throws up his hands.

"I should have known when I found the compass on the sand spit. We always begin with a directional guide. I was so sure she was off to find her own home that I forgot about that game pretty much."

I go on. "I didn't realize the name Van Rensselaer was a clue until the postmistress mentioned Rensselaerville. Then I knew Alice was telling me where she was going."

"You two sure make life complicated for yourselves up there in the woods."

"Lively," I reply. "Look here." I point to the map. "I'm right. Near the town is a waterfall and lots of acres for a pig to forage."

"Desdemondia," Bando says under his breath. "Well, if you are right, we should skip the pig farm. Alice won't be there."

"She won't. I'm sure of that. She's at that falls right now, climbing up a cascade or sitting in an air pocket under an overshoot."

We pack up the map and head for the road to Rensselaerville.

"I think we should stop at the pig farm, anyway," Bando says after a while.

"I'd rather go on," I say. "I'd like to find her before she's fined for having a pig on a nature preserve. The waterfall's on the Huyck Preserve. And we're tracking her to keep her out of scrapes, aren't we?"

"Nevertheless," Bando says, "I think we should talk to Hanni. It'll only take a minute to ask her if Alice told her where she is going. Hanni should still be there. The paper said the fair would last four days."

"Okay," I agree. "Maybe she left another clue with Hanni." We trek along in silence for about a mile.

"Sam," Bando suddenly says. "Want to watch the hacking tonight after we find Alice?"

"You bet I do," I answer. "Maybe there'll be some young peregrine falcons at hack."

The thought of seeing falcons on the wing lightens

my feet, and I step up our pace through the rugged farmland.

Along the way we talk about the weather and about the poor crops to our right and left, and finally we stop talking. Bando's brow is wrinkled, which means he's troubled. We walk on.

The uphill road plunges through a quaking aspen grove. A brown thrasher sits on a twig imitating all the birds in his area. I name them as he sings, "bluebird, cardinal, yellow-throated warbler." Then I whistle Frightful's name several times. It would be fun if he added that to his repertoire. There would be a bird in the Helderbergs who could call her name. I shake my head at the idea. I miss Frightful so much.

Around a bend, we see a large white farmhouse with Greek pillars, a barn, a silo, and a fenced yard where a dozen or so pickup and farm trucks are parked. Kids my age are everywhere.

"The Monroe Farm. Spotted Poland Chinas. Breeders." I read on the gatepost, then pause. A sumac bush has been deliberately cut and bent toward Rensselaerville. In the break is an acorn.

"Bando, I'm right," I say, pointing to Alice's woodland signature. "She's going to that falls."

We walk to the pig yard. A boy and a girl about my age are leaning on the fence, chatting, and I look down on the prettiest, cleanest pigs I've ever seen. I could almost like them.

I exchange hellos with them and ask for Hanni.

"She's in the first hog barn," the boy says, pointing. "Right over there."

"Come on, Bando."

"I'll stay here," Bando says. "You should talk to her alone. I'll study the pigs. I've never been this close to real pigs before."

I go in the barn where, after my eyes have adjusted to the dim light, I see a tall girl with bangs and shoulder-length soft brown hair crouched over a pig. She hears my steps and looks up.

"Hanni?"

"Hi."

She's pretty.

"Is Alice here?" I ask.

"Oh, you must be Sam." I nod. Her very blue eyes smile into mine. "She was expecting you, but she had to leave before you got here. She told me to tell you she was going ahead with the original plans you two made. She said you'd know what that meant."

"Oh, yes. The original plans," I say out loud while crying inside. What original plans?

"Good," I add, then take a deep breath, wondering if this is another Alice-clue.

"Did she take Crystal?" I ask, grasping for something to say.

"No, Crystal's here. Mr. Monroe will take care of her until Alice comes back."

"Oh, that's nice." I'm surprised to hear this *and* delighted. It's the first real news I've gotten. She's coming back to this farm.

"Where is Crystal?" I ask, trying to sound appropriately eager to see her. "I'd like to say hello. She's a neat pig." I think of Huck Finn again and feel myself blush.

"Crystal's in the third pen. Go talk to her. She's so lonely without Alice. Alice talked about how much you liked Crystal." Hanni looks smack into my eyes and smiles mischievously. There is a bolt of honesty skipping between us. She knows Alice likes to tell tall tales about me. I smile. I like her in her 4-H Club green shirt and trousers even if she does like pigs, or hogs, as they call them here.

"I'll be with you in a minute," she says.

I look in the third pen in despair. There are three pigs here. Which one is Crystal? I decide to leave before Hanni finds out I don't know, but she joins me.

"Sam," she says. "Pet little Crystal. Look at her, she's so sad." In vain I study the three spotted pigs to see which one is sad. They all have turned up mouths and seem to be completely happy.

"You *are* sad, aren't you Crystal?" Hanni says. I glance sidewise to see which pig she is looking at. Her lashes are so long I can't tell where her eyes are focused. I shift nervously from one foot to the other. I can't keep up this hoax much longer. I'm about to spoil Alice's story about my liking Crystal and come out with the truth when a pig with a white nose and black spots on her snout sniffs the air and runs toward me. I take a chance that she is recognizing the odor of her human family like all pets do—even members of the family they've never met. To all animals, even pollywogs, the family has a distinctive aroma, as distinctive as a clan plaid.

"Hello, Crystal," I say and pat the pig with the nose spots, hoping I'm right. The pig grunts expressively, and I scratch the bristly head. Hanni is smiling and watching the happy reunion. I am right.

Two other kids join us, but they are not interested in Crystal. They are staring at me, smiling, almost in deference. I am flattered, until I remember who I am, and when I do, want nothing more than to escape.

I back away, and just in time. Crystal is showing the tips of her tusks in warning. Having recognized the Gribley odor, this clever pig now knows something else about me. She knows I don't like pigs.

"Hanni," I say. "It's been nice to meet you. I want to thank you for all you did for Alice."

"It was fun, Sam Van Rensselaer," she says, and her eyes twinkle. She lowers her voice. "Did you understand the message? Do you know where she's going from here?"

"Yes," I reply. She tosses her hair with a flip of her head and smiles her beautiful smile. I wish it were for Sam Gribley, not Sam Van Rensselaer.

Then she winks and her eyes shine softly. She knows who I really am. The smile is for Sam Gribley.

With a couple of lilting strides, I join Bando. We take to the county road.

"Does she know where Alice is going?" he asks.

"Yes," I say, then stop stone still. I look at him sheepishly. "I forgot to ask her. She asked me."

"What did you say?"

"That I knew." I am blushing. I start off again.

"She *is* very pretty," Bando chides and sets his pace to mine.

"I did learn something," I tell him defensively.

"What's that?"

"Alice is coming back here."

"Good. We can take it easy," he says and slows down.

IN WHICH

The Dawn Breaks over Me

As we near Rensselaerville, we sit down in the shade of a white ash and plan what to do next.

I will go to the falls to see how Alice is. Bando will go to the library to find out where the hacking will be held on the vast preserve. That decided, we arise and I start off. Bando holds me back.

"You know, Sam," he says, "I've been thinking about

this hacking business in the paper. There's something strange about it. First of all, six o'clock in the evening is a bad time of day to hack a bird. My friend, Steve, at the peregrine mew, puts the fledglings out early in the morning so they'll have all day to look around and learn the environment before they fly off.

"And secondly, the news of the hacking wasn't on the front page like the pig show. It was in the paid personals. I think it was paid for because it's a message for one man, Skri, whoever he is. He was probably told to watch the newspaper for the date and place to meet."

"To hack birds?"

"I don't think they're hacking birds. I think it's a cover-up for something else. But I don't know what."

Bando turns to go, his black eyebrows pulled together in puzzlement.

"I'll meet you at the library," he calls.

"Okay," I reply, and, eager to see Alice, take off at a run down a dirt road, then cut over to Tenmile Creek, passing through a forest of yellow birch and maples. I follow the stream to the falls, a beauty that splashes down an eighty-foot staircase. The water hums, whispers, and spins white threads before pooling at the bottom.

This is it, I say to myself, this has to be where Alice is.

I jump down the rock staircase, pausing on ledges to look for signs of her camp, and come upon the ruins of

Alice's camp

an old mill. I poke around briefly, then go on to the bottom of the cascade. Finding no clues, I am on my way back up the falls when I see it.

"Alice's castle," I say, clambering up to a ledge where a stone wall with stones placed one on two, two on one, protects a natural cave from rain and wind.

I crawl in and give out a whoop. I've found her at last. Who else would make a bed of boughs and put a rabbit-skin pillow on it? Who else would have a container made out of two huge sycamore leaves sewn together with wild grapevine thread and filled with daylily buds?

My heart is beating as fast as a bird's. Alice is here, but she's also not here. She must be out foraging. I'll sit on the ledge and wait for her.

Now that I've found her what do I do?

When I started tracking her, I was only going to make sure she didn't get into a scrape. Since I know she's playing On the Track and we're supposed to find each other, I think I'll just hide until she comes back and say "Boo!" like she does when she finds me. Then I'll hug her.

To wait out of her sight, I climb into a young hemlock with limbs that hang over the falls and sit among the dense needles. From here I can see the creek, the gorge, and a pine plantation. From whichever direction Alice comes, I'll spot her.

As I settle in, I note that the sun has crossed the meridian. A yellow-shafted flicker chisels for an insect in a tree, and a kingfisher alights on an aspen bough. Alice has still not come back.

Suddenly the kingfisher screams his alarm note, and the forest becomes still. Wild eyes join mine, looking for the danger. Into the clearing below me slips a large eastern coyote. Gray as a wolf and almost as big, her movements are agile and swift. She lifts her head to inspect a scent on the wind. Her eyes are yellow fire.

I can't see her too well, but I can make out a large bird in her mouth.

This is the first eastern coyote I've ever seen, although Miss Turner said that this nearly extinct animal is making a comeback. Before the first settlers arrived in America, the big gray coyote of the woods lived and hunted all over the Northeast. With the cutting and burning of the forests for farming, its habitat was eliminated. Without the forest foods of ruffed grouse, turkeys, raccoons, and wood rats, the eastern coyote almost died out. Only a few lived on in the Adirondacks and the Catskill Mountains.

Then things turned around for woodland creatures. Like my mountain, the tilled land eroded and grew stones, not crops, and the farms were abandoned. The forests returned and the forest animal community returned with them, including the eastern coyote, which now ranges from Canada to the Bronx in New York City.

I sit perfectly still. Miss Turner said the eastern coyote is a clever hunter. Perhaps I can learn something from her.

The kingfisher keeps screaming his alarm cry but from a safe distance. The coyote ignores him, then moving so effortlessly she seems to float, she stops directly under me and drops the bird she is carrying. She teases it with her nose.

I lean forward and a branch snaps. The coyote vanishes, gray into green. Bird feathers ride the little whirlwind her passage stirred.

Annoyed at myself for scaring her, I settle back again and wait for Alice.

The shadows grow longer. A crow flies silently into a tree across the stream and, after checking the land and sky, drops to the ground near the coyote's prey. Cautiously it walks up to it and pecks. Suddenly there's a gray streak of coyote, a jaw snap, and the crow is dead.

She *is* a clever hunter. That bird was a trap.

Well, if that isn't neat. I'm going to do that, too. I take my sling and a stone from my pocket and move to a limb where I can swing my arm if another creature comes to the bait. I see the bird pretty well and it puzzles me. I come down lower. On its legs are jesses, swivel, and leash. Dropping to the ground, I pick up a sharp-shinned hawk.

The trappings are very professional, the bird fat and in good health. I wonder if this was one of the birds to be put at hack. It can't be. It's an adult. Only juveniles are hacked. It must belong to one of the hackers. He's brought her along to fly and exercise her.

I backtrack the coyote by following feathers and find that she killed her prey in a clearing not far from the falls. Feathers are scattered everywhere. I circle the area.

Whoever was here left sometime today. The dirt that put out the fire is still warm. I look around for a hacking

board. There is none, nor is there any indication that
there ever was one. But there *have* been birds of prey
here. There are holes in the ground, and a mark where
a perch fell and was dragged, probably by the coyote as
she went off with the sharp-shinned. All the perch holes
are circled with claw marks. A tethered raptor will
make marks like these. When frightened or restless,
they fly to the end of the leash, drop to the ground, and
tear the earth with their talons. Frightful made such a
circle around her perch before she felt comfortable with
me.

I find the clinching proof that raptors have been here.
Falcons, hawks, and owls swallow fur, bones, and feathers as well as meat, then regurgitate, or "cast," the
unused parts in tidy pellets. There are castings near the
perch holes.

This has to be the site of the hacking, but why isn't
anyone here? Did the coyote scare them off? I guess so.
I'd sure move if a coyote killed one of my birds.

I go back to the falls. Alice is still not here. I'm beginning to think she's gone fishing or berrying and will not
return until dusk. It's about four o'clock. Time to find
Bando.

Putting the jesses, leash, and ring in my belt pouch,
I follow Tenmile Creek to the bridge and climb the
abutment. At the top I get my first look at Rensselaerville.

It's pretty, but more so is a working water mill right
across the road. Eagerly I circle it. The waterwheel itself

is housed in a huge shed built against the milling room, which is two stories high.

Boy, can I learn a lot here! A huge, wonderful, operating water mill. As I round the building I find an old millstone. That tells me this is a gristmill, not a sawmill, and it tells me the mill is old. The stone is dressed with circular furrows, a design that hasn't been used for more than a hundred years. The furrows move the ground flour out into the vat.

I walk around the mill again then go to the front door, certain I'm going to be disappointed, for I have not seen a person or heard the wheel turn since I arrived. I am right. A sign on the door reads: HOURS: 12–5 SAT–SUN, MID-MAY THROUGH LABOR DAY. GRIST MILL 1789.

"It's Tuesday," I say to the door and knock anyway. No one answers. It's just as well. I haven't time for this right now. I've got to tell Bando that I've found Alice's camp and a site where falconers, if not the hackers, have been.

I hurry down the main street, which is lined with wooden houses painted white, yellow, blue, and red. Some look to be as old as the mill. Behind them rise the steeples of several churches. Enormous maples and spruces shade the sidewalks. Like Livingstonville, this is a very quiet town. There is no one but me on the street.

I come to a Tudor town house with RENSSELAERVILLE LIBRARY AND READING ROOM hand lettered under the gable. I open the door.

Bando is at an antique reading desk, engrossed in a book. I slip up quietly and sit down beside him.

"Find out about the hacking?" He startles and looks up.

"Not yet. I've been wandering around town waiting for the library to reopen. It's not a busy place. The hours are eight to eleven and four thirty to six. The librarian just opened the doors again."

"I've found Alice," I whisper.

"You have?" His face lights up.

"Well, yes and no. I've found her camp. She wasn't there, but she'll be back. She's made a fine stone-walled camp. Quite permanent."

"In that case," he says, closing his book, "let's celebrate by going across the street for an early dinner. At the grocery store where I stopped for a newspaper, I heard that the chef is marvelous."

"Aw, come on Bando," I say. "I don't like fancy places. Besides I have dried venison and horse sorrel for dinner." He's unmoved. I try another temptation. "Let's eat by the waterfall and wait for Alice."

"I can wait more patiently over good restaurant food." He shoulders his packbasket. "We won't be long."

"I haven't got any money."

"My treat. You've treated me all along the way. Now it's my turn."

"I found where the hackers have been. Don't you want to see?"

He looks interested when I say that.

"Are they there?"

"No."

"Then I'll see it later."

Reluctantly I follow Bando to the library door. As I pass the checkout desk, I stop. A book entitled *Goshawk,* by T. H. White, is in the return box. I thumb through it, for although I have read it many times, I can always read it again. It's about the training and manning of the spirited, fighting goshawk.

"Would you like to take the book out?" asks the librarian, a scholarly looking man who is settling down in his chair to work.

"No, thank you," I say. "Not today."

"There's been quite a bit of interest in hawks and falcons around here lately," he says.

"Any particular reason?" Bando asks.

"There have been falconers around," he says, stroking his beard. "Just a few weeks ago two men offered my son, Eric, a couple of hundred dollars to locate a sharp-shinned hawk nest for them."

"Did he do it?"

"No, he was afraid they would harm the birds. The conservation officer, who is rooming across the street this week—he moves around from town to town—told Eric there was a renewed interest in hawks and falcons since some of them have been designated endangered species.

"They're precious, and precious things are worth a

lot of money—like the nearly extinct white rhinos of Africa. Poachers make fortunes selling their horns. Terrible." Bando is moving toward the door, but the librarian is not finished.

"Look at this," he says and walks over to the community bulletin board.

"Two men put this up when I opened this morning." He points to a card.

"Skri," it reads. "Hacking moved to Beaver Corners, dawn of the 26th. Go to church. Bate." In the left-hand corner are some Arabic letters.

"That's interesting," comments Bando.

"See that," the librarian taps the letters. "That was put there just before eleven. A well-dressed man drove up in a green car and came in. He read the note and signed it."

"Hmm," Bando says. "Probably acknowledging he's read it."

"He was chatty," the librarian goes on. "Talked to me for quite a while—said he was from Saudi Arabia. He thumbed through the goshawk book, too. Said the sheik he worked for had a goshawk.

"The Arab sheiks prize falcons," the librarian continues. "They've been practicing the art of falconry for thousands of years. I understand they'll pay more for a falcon than a racing car, especially since that pesticide DDT got in the food chain and wiped out so many of the birds of prey."

"They'll pay high prices?" Bando says.

"Selling falcons to Arabian sheiks," the librarian goes on, "has always been a big business, even when Jesus lived."

Bando opens the door. "We're going across the street to the restaurant. If you hear or see anything more about the hacking, we'd sure like to know."

"All right. I think the two men will come back to see if their note has been read and signed. And by the way," he goes on, "the men who put up the note are the same ones who wanted Eric to find them a sharp-shinned hawk nest. They're in town. Eric and I saw them as we came down the road just now." He looks at me. "You were at the mill, and they were walking up the creek, of all things."

Bando reads the posted card once more and shakes his head.

"Let's dine," he says. "I need to think, and I think best over food."

"Okay," I say, "but I sure want to surprise Alice when she comes home. Let's eat fast."

As I enter this restaurant, I am prepared to shrink into the furniture, but it's nice. The room is bright and pleasant. One wall is a grocery store, where coffee, canned soups, bread, and pancake mixes are stacked on shelves. The kitchen is on the other side of a large, pass-through window. Two young men in chef hats are consulting over the stove. It's early, around 5:00 P.M., but there are already two couples at a table near the window. The food must be good. I sit down and pick up the menu.

"Squab with sorrel sauce," I read aloud. "Smoked eel on a bed of wild asparagus."

"Desdemondia," groans Bando. "Wouldn't you know I'd hit a restaurant that specializes in game and wild foods. I'm back on the trail again."

One of the chefs, a large man with rosy jowls, comes to our table and introduces himself as Mr. Milo, the head chef and owner of the restaurant.

He addresses Bando. "The Cajun opossum with wild rice is superb."

"I have my heart set on filet mignon," Bando states. "Don't you have steak?"

"Well, yes," he answers reluctantly. "But the leg of wild rabbit with tarragon sauce is much better." Bando rolls his eyes and orders the steak.

"I'll take the wild rabbit," I say, then add, "have you ever tried it on a bed of daylily buds?"

"Daylilies? No, I've never even tasted them, but I hear they're a great delicacy."

"I have some with me if you would like to try them." I take a leaf bag from my belt pouch. "Moisten them in egg and roll them in flour—preferably acorn flour—and fry them."

"Thank you very much," he says and sniffs their tart odor.

"Mr. Milo," Bando says. "If you're interested in wild

delicious

Daylily

foods, speak with my friend Sam here. He's an expert."

"He is?" He turns to me. "Can I talk to you later?"
I nod and he writes down our orders.

"I'd like that steak very rare," Bando says, and Mr.
Milo turns to go, then leans down to me.

"I have mulled sumac tea," he says. "Would you like
some?"

"I sure would."

When the marvelous meal is consumed, we step out
of the restaurant and into the late afternoon light just as

a pickup camper pulls up to the library. A man gets out and hurries inside, leaving another man sitting at the wheel with the motor running. They must be the two men the librarian suspected would be back to see if their note on the bulletin board had been read and initialed.

We are crossing the street when the man comes out of the library.

"Bando," I say, pointing. "That's Officer Longbridge!"

"That man?" he says. "He's not Leon Longbridge." The man hears us, looks up, and jumps in the pickup. The door slams and the car speeds off.

"He *is* Leon Longbridge," I say. "He's the man who confiscated Frightful. He has one blue eye and one brown eye."

"He may be the man who confiscated Frightful, but he's not Leon."

I feel sick. I went to Delhi to find out if the conservation officer was named Leon Longbridge, but I didn't think to look at him.

"Sam," Bando's voice is urgent. "That man has Frightful, and he's about to sell her. He's no hacker. Let's find the conservation officer and get to Beaver Corners now."

"I'm not coming," I say.

Bando spins around and stares at me. "Don't you want to get Frightful back?"

"Yes, yes," I answer. "But Alice camped near those

hackers and the librarian saw them going up Tenmile Creek a little while ago. I'm going back to find her."

"Yes, do!" he says forcefully. "Go find Alice."

I borrow the Westerlo and Altamont quadrangle maps and we separate, planning to meet at Beaver Corners at dawn if all is well.

IN WHICH

I Am On the Track

I run down the street, vault over the bridge railing, and climb down the abutment to the creek. I take off my moccasins and, wading into the cool water, splash upstream toward Alice's camp.

I'm a tug-of-war inside. I want to look for Frightful with all my heart, and with all my heart I want to find Alice. But the battle, my head says, is already won. I've got to find Alice.

Some things become clear as I run. Frightful was stolen from me. And Bate, who must be that blue-and-brown-eyed man, is going to sell her to Skri at Beaver Corners. Hacking is just a code word that means Bate has birds to sell.

What isn't clear is Alice's situation. Did the two men find her? Did they harm her? I run faster.

With the beginning of twilight darkening the falls, I splash up to Alice's camp.

She should be here, but she's not. Where is she? Feeling prickles of fear running over my skin, I crawl into her stone home and sit down.

I am paralyzed. I can't seem to act. I don't know what to do. Should I wait? Or should I get the police? In anguish I roll over and bury my face in her rabbit-fur pillow.

It crackles. I snatch it up and find a letter. Crawling out on the ledge, my hands trembling, I lay a small pile of pine needles and twigs, then, taking out my flint and steel, strike a spark and start a fire. As the flame flares up, my heart thumps like a plumping mill. Why is she writing me a letter? That's not part of On the Track. She must be in trouble. I unfold a sheet of paper with the Monroe Poland China Farm crest on it and see it is dated this morning. The letter was here when I arrived before noon, but since I didn't lie down on the pillow I didn't find it.

"Hi, Sam," I read. "Isn't this fun?"

Fun? Are you crazy? I am worried to death about you, Alice, and you think this is fun. Don't you know that dangerous men are around you? I hold the letter closer to the fire and read on.

"There were falconers here in the woods. I saw them. They left about an hour ago, soon after the nice woodland coyote killed one of their birds.

"I have some good news for you. But I can no longer wait for you to get here to tell you. You're too pokey. I'm off to the Helderberg Escarpment."

She's gone. She departed after the men left the woods and before they came up the creek. She's all right. Maybe they didn't even see her. I breathe a sigh of relief and read on.

"There's a leaf bag of hickory nuts on the ledge above the bed. Help yourself. The coyote has puppies under the rhododendron bush by the old mill. Let's get a coyote puppy; they're adorable. Signed,

"Your friend, Alice Van Rensselaer. Ha. Wasn't it fun having everyone bow and scrape because they thought you were a Van Rensselaer? People-clues work when you give them to nice people like Mr. and Mrs. Van Sandtford and Hanni. Hanni's neat.

Alice."

I groan and smile at the same time. "You're impossible."

Now that I know she's all right I'm angry at her. I haven't got time for her little games with sun compasses, pigs, Van Rensselaers, and coyotes. I've got a sawmill to tend and food to gather for the winter.

Alice, will you ever grow up and think of someone besides yourself?

But I am on the move. Alice is safe. I should have

known when I saw that eight-hundred-foot drop off the Helderberg Escarpment that she was headed for that falls from the moment she left her tree house.

Now, to go to Beaver Corners and get my beloved falcon back.

I stamp out the fire, bury the charred twigs, and sprinkle the burned spot with dirt. As the full moon comes over the tips of the hemlocks in the east and the sun goes down in the west, I climb down the falls and splash toward the bridge.

A dark mass to my left attracts my attention; something dull in texture is floating on the surface of the darkening stream. I wade to it.

"Oh, no," I wail.

It's the mother coyote. That's what the men were going to do when they headed up the creek, kill the coyote. They came back to seek revenge. Near the mother floats a puppy, and I can look no more. These men are cruel—and they have Frightful.

I splash down the creek, climb to the bridge, and put on my moccasins.

I don't even glance at the gristmill, but go straight to the restaurant.

The evening diners, a well-dressed group, are chatting and waiting to be served. I walk as casually as I can to the kitchen, where Mr. Milo is checking a dish in the oven.

"Mr. Milo," I say, trying to be calm. "Where's the police station?"

"There's no police station in Rensselaerville," he says. "Why? What's up?"

"Two men are about to sell my falcon to an agent for an Arab sheik. They're at Beaver Corners near East Berne and should be arrested. It's a felony to hold endangered species, and it must be worse to sell them."

"The nearest police are about twenty miles from here in Altamont," Mr. Milo says, his eyes wide. "I'll call Sean Conklin, our conservation officer. He's been staying in town. He can make arrests."

Mr. Milo dials his number and gets no answer.

"Good," I say. "He and Bando must have gone to Beaver Corners."

"Anything I can do?" Mr. Milo asks. "My buyer is going there in the morning to purchase red raspberries from a farm. He can give you a ride."

"No, thanks," I say. "It's only about twelve miles and there's a full moon tonight. I'm on my way."

"Suit yourself," he says and I hurry off.

At the last streetlight on the road out of town, I take out the map with the Helderberg Escarpment on it. Alice is probably already there. I study the contours and names. Most likely she's near the Indian Ladder where Outlet Falls plunges off the cliff. Miss Turner said that once the Indians felled a tree against the escarpment. The stumps of its branches, which they had trimmed away, formed the rounds of the ladder they climbed to the top. Now, she said, wooden and iron steps take its place.

I start off for Beaver Corners in the last light of day,
happy that Alice is far from the men who have Frightful, but keeping an eye out for piled stones or corncob
arrows to say for certain that she is.

The road winds through farmland that looks like a
rough quilt in the glow of the rising moon. Lights go off
in a lonely house at the end of the macadam, and I'm on
a dirt road.

Bats swing over my head and nighthawks cry as I
hurry along. The freshness of the countryside and the
knowledge that Alice is safe sends me whistling on my
way to find Frightful.

Almost all the lights are out in the little town of
Berne as I come down a steep road to its main street.
One streetlight is burning above a historical marker
and, knowing I don't have to reach Beaver Corners
before dawn, I stop and read it.

"The Anti-rent War began here in 1839. The farmers
of the Helderberg Mountains declared they would no
longer pay rent to the Van Rensselaers and honor leases
which bound their land forever and forever, for an annual payment, to a landed aristocracy.

"The rent was ten to fourteen bushels of wheat, four
fat fowls, and one day's service each year with team and
wagon. The tenant had to pay the taxes and build and
maintain the roads. The patroon reserved all water
and mineral rights. After two hundred years without
being permitted to own the land they had opened and

worked, the tenant farmers rebelled. Dressed as Indians, they harassed the Van Rensselaer agents and the state militia when they came into the mountains to collect the rent. The militia fought back. The war went on for thirteen years, the legal struggle for ownership for another twenty-four. Finally, one hundred years after the Declaration of Independence, the Supreme Court ruled against the Van Rensselaers."

The rent seemed like a lot to me, if the land was anything like Great-grandfather Gribley's. Ten to fourteen bushels of wheat would have been most of his crop.

As I cross a bridge and head toward East Berne, which is about two miles from Beaver Corners, I see the ruins of an old water mill. It, too, is illuminated by a streetlight. With only a couple of hours of walking ahead of me, and it being hours before dawn, I take time out to look at the mill. There is not much left of it. The stones in the crumbled walls (they must not have been laid one on two, two on one) are soft with moss. There are no millstones around. It must have been a sawmill. That's neat.

I look for rusty machinery, shafts, and bolts that I might use, find none, and turn to go when an out-of-character structure on the sluice wall attracts my attention. It's a pile of stones two on one, one on two. Alice, I say. She's passed by. All is well. She's left me a message at a place she knows I'll stop—an old water mill.

Alice's sundial

I smile. On the Track is very satisfying—when it's going right.

The moon shines on her structure, and I get down on my knees to try to figure out what she's saying. Two large rocks support a thin triangular stone in an upright position. Thirteen pebbles are arranged in an arc. It's a sundial. She's telling me what time she was here. I look closer. A stick is laid on the two-hour. The sun was up. She was here this afternoon at two. Good, I say. She's sleeping by the falls right now.

I'm about to start off again when I decide to use the moon and Alice's dial to find out what time it is. When the moon is full, which it is tonight, it is directly opposite the sun, so the shadow it casts will give me the correct time. I look down. It's eleven o'clock.

I'm about six miles from Beaver Corners, and the men won't be there until dawn. I think I have time to grab a little sleep before I go on. I'm pretty tired.

Several hours later, I awake in alarm—have I overslept? I jump up, look at Alice's dial, and am relieved to see it's only 3:00 A.M. The moon is beginning to slide west. I orient myself by facing it. My right arm points north. Beaver Corners is northeast of me. I start off in that direction, set a swift pace, and cover the four miles in a little more than an hour. Two to go.

East Berne is a smaller town than Livingstonville. It doesn't even have a gas station, and the post office is a trailer. I like it but do not linger.

I take the road to Beaver Corners, pass several dark houses and a church, and then I'm out in the wilds again. Miles of dark swampland lie to either side of the road. Frog songs and owl calls hang like a sound blanket over this lowland. I jog along, watching for bobcats and beaver—even black bear.

I arrive at Beaver Corners as the eastern sky begins to lighten. There's not much here, a crossroad, woodland, and an abandoned church that looks like it's ready to fall down. I don't see Bando or the conservation officer's car, but recalling the note on the library wall, I cross the road to the church.

As I walk, I whistle for Frightful, a birdlike call in the night. If she's here, she'll answer me.

She does not.

I round the abandoned church and find Bate's pickup. They're here, but not in the truck. I peer through the camper window. Frightful's not there, either, but I do see falcon perches, leashes, and hoods. She's near. I run around the church. She's not staked out, so I look for her in the woods. As I come down a slope, I see a green car parked in the tall grass near a beaver dam.

It must be the agent's car. I look through the side window but see only seats.

I despair. Maybe the coyote killed Frightful before she killed the sharp-shinned. Alice didn't mention Frightful at all. I poke my head in the church and wonder why they ever decided to meet here. The place is falling in and very dangerous. Boards creak and the floor is ripped up and gaping. Where are the men, where are the birds? They're around here somewhere.

I walk deeper in the woods in search of them, give up the hunt, and return to the other side of the road to wait for Bando and Officer Conklin.

I see nothing but nature and hear nothing but nature.

When it's light enough to read the maps, I take out the Altamont quadrangle and look at Beaver Corners. There's a cave marked on it, just about where I am sitting. Maybe that's where the men are.

Poking around, I push back some tall rushes and find a path leading right up to the cave.

The entrance is narrow, the cavern black. I climb a

pine and knock off an old limb stub rich in resin. On the ground I start a small fire with my flint and steel and light the knot. When it flares up, I slip between two huge slabs of limestone and sidle down the tight tunnel. Suddenly I am in a high, narrow room. This is great. Water trickles down the walls; a bat comes in for the day and hangs upside down on the pointed ceiling above me. I hold my torch high and see three long, narrow passageways leading into the dark underworld. This doesn't look like a good meeting place, but a cave is a cave. It screams out to be explored, and I go on. Walking down one of the tunnels, I turn a corner and am looking out on the beaver dam and the agent's car. The cave has two entrances. I go back and take the middle passage. It ends.

I might as well go down the last passage. Bending low, I inch along. The pine knot flares and throws off so much black smoke I do not see a fourth passageway on my left. I pass it. The tunnel I'm in dwindles to two feet, and I turn back.

As I return, I see the tunnel I missed minutes ago. It is wide and high enough for me to walk in upright. I ease myself along, intrigued by the smooth, waterworn walls.

Far ahead a light shines. This is not the blue white light of day but a yellow electric light. Walking toward it, I see that it is coming through a crack in the boards of a big door. I hear voices. Quietly I approach and peer through the crack.

I can see only half of a basement which, I judge from the distance I've come, is under the church. A man steps into my vision—it's Bate. He's holding a leash in one hand, and probably Frightful in the other, but I can't see that hand. My heart beats so hard it shakes my shirt. Let it be Frightful. Let it be Frightful.

I move slightly so I can see the other half of the room—and my spirits sink. Bate is holding, not Frightful, but a prairie falcon. Bate's driver is standing beside him. Seated on a barrel is the man who must be the agent, Skri.

"We made a deal for a peregrine falcon," Skri says. "I won't pay fifty thousand dollars for a prairie falcon. No. No. And where is the sharp-shinned?"

I have seen and heard enough. Biting my lips to keep from crying, I pick up my pine knot and return to the road and the dawn.

Something terrible has happened to Frightful. I don't even care if the men are arrested or not. She's dead; I know.

A car drives up, stops, and Dando jumps out.

"Hi, Sam." he says. "Officer Conklin and I came here last night, but no one was around."

"There is now," I say as Officer Conklin comes around his car and introduces himself. He is a tall, bony-faced man with a mustache and a lot of red hair. He carries a revolver on his hip. The work of an environmental conservation officer is serious.

"Where are they?" he asks, looking around.

"In the basement of that church," I answer. "But you can't get there through the church; it's falling down. The cave across the road leads into it."

"The old Tenant Hideout," he says in surprise. "The farmers of the Helderbergs went into the church basement and hid in this cave when the rent collectors and the militia came after them. Not many people know about it now. Just local kids and a few spelunkers.

"I'll hide my car off the road in the woods," he says, "and we'll wait in the bushes for the men to come out."

"It's no use, sir." I say. "You can't arrest them. They don't have my peregrine falcon. She's dead."

"If they are selling hawks and falcons, I can arrest them," Sean Conklin replies. "Birds of prey are protected by three different laws, one of which is a multinational treaty endorsed by 103 members. Fines run up to $250,000.

"I've been after these fellows for a long time," he goes on. "They are not licensed falconers and should not be keeping these birds, and for sure not selling them."

We walk around the church to the pickup, and I show him the green car by the beaver dam. Bando tells him that the librarian saw the man called Skri drive off in such a car.

Officer Conklin puts a foot on the steps of the church. Boards rattle and creak.

"They surely won't come out this way," he says. "Let's wait by the cave entrance."

Hardly has he spoken than we see Bate and his friend coming across the road toward us. They have no birds at all. Conklin can't arrest them. They're going to walk away free.

"Hello, Conklin," Bate calls jauntily.

"Hello, Bate."

Helpless to act, he watches them go around the church to their pickup. Then I think of the cave. "Don't let them get away," I say. "Bando, come with me."

I dash through the woods to the green car just as Skri, carrying the hooded prairie falcon on his fist, comes out of the beaver-dam cave exit and runs to his car. I swing my sling over my head, aiming for the car door, and strike it a thundering blow. Skri jumps. The bird flaps.

"Stop where you are, mister," Sean Conklin calls. "You're under arrest." Seeing the revolver, Skri quietly walks toward him.

"It's his bird," he says, pointing to Bate.

Officer Conklin turns to Bate. "If that is so, you'd better come with me, too. You are not on the roster of licensed falconers."

"Where is my peregrine falcon?" I cry. "What did you do to her?"

He does not answer.

"You didn't take her to the university, did you? She's dead, isn't she?"

He does not answer.

"The man's not going to talk, Sam," Officer Conklin says. "He'll incriminate himself."

I turn away in despair, and Bando slips his arm around my shoulder. I shrug him off and walk to the edge of the woods. Sitting down, I put my elbows on my knees and my chin in my fists. I swallow hard. I had been so sure I would find Frightful here.

After a while Officer Conklin walks over to me.

"Sam," he says. "We're taking the men to Altamont to book them. Do you want to come?"

"No, no, I don't, thank you," I answer. "I'm going to the Helderberg Escarpment."

"Let me shake your hand," he says, extending his right hand. "Your quick thinking saved the prairie falcon."

I look up. Bando is holding the hooded falcon and smiling at her. She is a beauty.

"Sam," he says. "Sean Conklin needs me to carry the falcon while he drives these men to Altamont. After he has booked them, he and his son will take the bird to New Paltz. There's a licensed falconer at the university who will ship her to Boise, Idaho, where another falconer will meet her. He'll hack her back to freedom in her native habitat."

I am listening intently.

"He says there is a network of falconers who use their knowledge to keep these birds flying."

"That's what falconry is today," Officer Conklin

adds. "Falconers working for the birds of prey, not the birds of prey working for falconers."

"Are you sure you don't want to come along? Then we can start home."

"I'm going to get Alice," I say. "She's at the big falls on the escarpment. We'll be there if you decide to join us."

With my hands in my pocket and my head bowed, I take the road to the Helderberg Escarpment and to the water that spills eight hundred feet.

"The goshawks," I say, breaking into a run. I had forgotten all about them. It's the end of June. They'll have young. The eggs hatch around the first week in June, and the nestlings are ready to fledge in early July. During this time the parents are very dangerous. Their parental instincts are at their height, and they defend their offspring with strikes and slicing talons. Frightful's parents were docile compared to these birds, and they were fierce enough. They nearly knocked me off the cliff.

I run faster, for as sure as my name is Sam Gribley, Alice will climb that tree to see the nestlings. And as sure as her name is Alice Gribley, she'll end up on the ground or badly cut or both.

IN WHICH

A Bird Talks to Me

The sun is just hitting the tops of the trees when I find a well-marked trail to the big falls and take off along it.

I hear the cry of a goshawk and look up. Recognizing the female by her great size, I stop running to admire the silver gray body streaking through the sky. She is carrying a rabbit home to her nestlings in her taloned feet.

I keep her in view as I follow her toward the falls. Suddenly she screams the alarm cry of the goshawk. Her mate appears in the sky, seemingly coming from nowhere, and dives straight down at me. I must be near the nest.

I am. High in the spruce tree in front of me is a large nest of sticks and—climbing up toward it—Alice.

There she is. Her yellow hair sticks straight up as she lifts a wiry leg and places it on a limb.

The female goshawk climbs, positions herself above Alice, and dives.

"Alice!" I yell. "Duck."

With her wings snapping to gain speed, the great bird aims for Alice, who ducks her head just in time. The female shoots over the treetops, turns, and comes screaming back. The gleaming scimitars that are her talons slice the air just above Alice's head.

"Alice," I shout again. "Get down here."

"Sam!" She looks down and laughs happily.

"You're going to get hurt!" I holler angrily.

"She can't hit me," Alice answers and leans out to see me better. "There're too many limbs." The spruce tree is densely limbed and needled, but what Alice doesn't know is that a goshawk can maneuver a maze.

The frantic hawk speeds upward and, catching a downdraft, hurtles herself at Alice again.

"Here she comes!"

Alice pulls a limb across her body. The hawk dodges it and flies off. Once more Alice leans out to look down at me.

"Sam, hi. I knew you'd find me."

"Alice, get down here. That bird is dangerous."

"I'm okay. I won't let her hit me." She brandishes a spruce branch to show me how she fends the bird off.

"Please."

"Not yet." She climbs higher. The female screams an alarm which is answered by the tercel, who instantly appears and dive-bombs Alice.

Three crows hear the alarm and fly out of the woods to harass the goshawks. Cawing frantically, the crows pursue. To them, any bird of prey must be harassed, but goshawks must be unmercifully bedeviled. They caw without letup.

The tercel ignores them and climbs, it seems to me, into the very stratosphere. Somewhere out of sight he

turns and comes into view, plunging straight down at
my sister. She flattens herself her against the tree. This
is crazy.

"Come down, Alice!"

"No."

Concerned now, I take a running start, jump, grab
the first limb of the spruce, and find myself kicking
wildly to fend off the female goshawk.

Alice climbs higher. I climb after her. The red eyes of
the tercel flash as he comes at me. I pull down a branch.
He veers, screams, and speeds off. After wiping spruce
dust out of my eyes, I look up to see Alice practically in
the nest.

"Sam, come look at the babies."

I can't believe what she's doing. Miss Turner told her
what happened to people who went near goshawk nests.

"Get down before you're knocked down," I shout
and climb faster.

Alice doesn't come down. I can barely see her for the
dense limbs, but I do see the parent goshawks. They
scream and dive, but do not hit her.

I watch and wait, not daring to climb any higher. The
limbs that hold the nest are too small to support both
Alice and me.

The nestlings call their wheezy notes. The parents
swoop. Finally, Alice starts down, and I lower myself
on the ladder of limbs, looking up as I go to make sure
she's coming. Through the needles, I see three baby

goshawks peering over the side of the nest. Their mouths are open in fury.

The tercel circles the tree and grows calmer as we descend.

I drop to the ground, followed by Alice. The female alights on the top of a dead tree, panting from fatigue and fear. Her beak is open, her tongue thrust out. She lowers her wings to attack again. What courage.

I pull Alice across the clearing into the shelter of the forest understory. Out of breath, we stop and look at each other.

"Where have you been?" she asks.

"Where have I been? Alice—!" What can I say? "You've got a cut on your head," is all I can think of, so I say it.

Taking out some leaves of the horse sorrel I had picked for last night's meal, I wipe away the blood. The Iroquois Indians used the leaves and roots of this plant to stop bleeding and purify cuts. The bleeding does stop.

"You look like a war veteran," I say, throwing my arms around both her and her pack.

"Be careful," she says, pulling away.

The goshawks have located us and are circling above the trees. I take Alice's hand and pull her to the edge of the escarpment, where I had seen a ledge about ten feet down. I scramble to it and reach up to help her. She slides to my side.

We find ourselves on a ledge under an overhang. I push Alice far under it.

"Get back there where the birds can't see you," I say, urging her deeper into the cavelike shelter.

"Be careful," she snaps. "You're jabbing the baby."

"What *are* you talking about?"

Taking off her pack she opens it and gently lifts a screaming, fighting baby goshawk.

"What are you doing with that?" I shout.

"Sam, don't be mad." The fierce nestling clenches her talons on air. "I got her for you. When I read your note saying Frightful had been confiscated, I cried. Then I remembered the goshawks Miss Turner had told us about. So I got you one."

"Oh, Alice." That's all I can say.

I have accused her of everything from being selfish to stubborn. I have even wanted to send her home. And now she has gotten me this priceless gift. I take the wild-eyed hawklet in my hands and, holding her feet-out, bury my face in her sweet birdy-smelling feathers.

"Oh, Alice, she's beautiful."

"*Eeeck,*" cries the bird, turns her head, and clamps her hooked beak on my hand. Alice pulls her work gloves from her pack and hands them to me. She took them, I now see, to handle a goshawk. She gave a lot of thought to this adventure.

Putting on the gloves, I hold the screaming warrior at arm's length.

Alice's gift

"What a present, Alice. What a wonderful present."
Gently rolling the little goshawk on her back, I stroke
her breast to hypnotize her and calm her down. She
looks at me. I look at her and fall in love. She has large
eyes, a Persian beak, and gray silver feathers. Her eyes
are just turning red like her parents'. Wrapping her
carefully in my T-shirt so she can't see, thrash, and hurt
herself, I place her far back under the overhang where
she can recover from the scare of being handled by
people.

"I'm going up for water, Alice. The little bird is
thirsty." She hands me our leather carrier.

"You rest," I say. She nods and sits down grinning happily but apparently glad to obey for a change.

I climb to the top of the escarpment. Not far away a stream flows out of a limey cave, rushes to the edge, and plunges off. I watch its breathless descent.

Maybe Alice wasn't coming here to see this waterfall, I say to myself as the wild stream shoots off into space, but I'm sure glad she did. I stand and admire it in silence and am soothed by the sight of the falling water.

I fill the water bag and am starting back when a squirrel runs over the leaves. I load my sling and, twirling it above my head, let go of one string. The animal falls dead.

At last, victory on the first shot. Maybe Alice and I *can* survive on my mountain after all. I pick up the squirrel and a brown paper bag dropped by a hiker, then look around for a meadow environment. I find it, a clearing made by campers. As if I am in a familiar grocery store, I look along the meadow edge until I see what I've come for—the delicious leaves of the lamb's-quarters. I also check out a moist pocket by the stream for groundnuts and am rewarded with a string of three-inch nuts on the roots of one plant. I take the nuts and replant the roots.

I am rich again. I have Alice, a squirrel, groundnuts, and greens. I climb down to our camp. Alice is hugging her knees and looking out over the valley below.

"Sam," she says. "Let's stay here a few days. It's beautiful. Look at the view." Needless to say, I hadn't noticed the view, but out before us lie mountains, villages, and rivers. The Adirondacks rise like a jagged blue cutout in the far distance, and off to the right Outlet Falls shoots out over the ledge and spins a white trail to the rocks below.

Groundnut

"Good idea," I say. "It's the perfect place for you and me. I'm close to a goshawk's nest, and you're next to a mighty waterfall."

After making a small fire, I cut the paper bag with the scissors in Alice's Swiss Army knife and fold it into a box. In it I put the lamb's-quarters and water and place

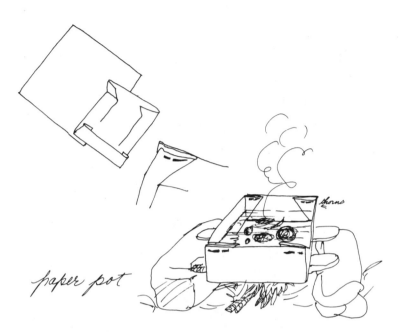

paper pot

it directly on the fire. The paper won't burn, because the water keeps it below its kindling point. You can do this with leaves too. The squirrel I cook on a spit.

"Alice," I say after we have eaten. "We have to return the little bird."

"No, Sam, no."

"It's illegal to have her."

"No, it's not. It's a hawk, not a falcon."

"Goshawks are protected by law, too. Sean Conklin, the conservation officer, said all the birds of prey are protected under the International Migratory Bird Treaty. They belong to the world."

"Oh, Sam, no. I came so far to get the little bird for you."

"I know it," I say. "Boy, do I know it." I look at her.

Mother was right to let Alice stay on the mountain. Living with nature teaches you to give. Alice would not have thought of doing something for me when she first came to my wilderness home.

"Please, don't take her back," Alice pleads. "Not now."

"Well, not right away. We'll enjoy her until dark. Tonight, when the goshawks can't see, I'll return her to her parents."

Alice shakes her head sadly.

"You'll feel good," I tell her, "knowing the little bird will take her place in the wild scheme of things."

"No, I won't. I want you to have a goshawk."

I uncover the quiet nestling, who, small as she is, picks a battle with me, a giant. She stabs and grips the glove. Carefully unlocking her strong talons, I place her on the ground and offer her a drink and a squirrel part I saved for her. She eats ravenously, and sadly I think of Frightful when she was this age. Then I cover the little bird again and put her far back under the overhang. Thrilled by the privilege of just holding a baby goshawk, I step lightly to the edge of our hideout.

"Creee, creee, creee, car-reet."

I grab Alice's arm.

"Did you hear that?"

"Frightful!" she gasps.

We scramble to the top of the escarpment. Shooting across the clouds like a crossbow in the sky speeds a peregrine falcon. No other bird has that profile.

"Creee, creee, creee, car-reet." And no other bird but Frightful knows my peregrine name.

"Frightful," I call. I can barely see her for the mist in my eyes. She is coming toward us, pumping her wings with quick, strong strokes. Three feet from my face she calls my name again, swoops up, and "waits on" just above me.

"Creee, creee, creee, car-reet." Frightful drops lower, hovers in front of me, then climbs away. She goes higher and higher until she is out of sight.

"She's free, Alice, she's free."

"I knew that."

"What do you mean, you knew that?"

"I told you in my note that I had some good news for you, didn't I? Well, that's it. I set Frightful free."

"You did?"

"I found her in the Rensselaerville woods. I cut off her jesses. That's better than her going to the university, isn't it?"

"Tell me again. What did you do?"

"Cut her jesses."

I whoop in joy, sweep her up in my arms, and hug her.

"How did it happen?"

"Well, while I was foraging near the Rensselaerville falls, I walked into a clearing where there were three tethered falcons. One of them was Frightful. I recognized her by the jesses and leash you made. No one was there, so I cut her free. That's all."

"Alice," I close my eyes in thanks.

"Then," she continues, "while I was standing very still, watching her on the top of a tree getting her bearings, the coyote slipped up and killed one of the other birds. I stood perfectly still. She didn't see me because she was too busy trying to carry the bird off. It was tethered and she couldn't run off with it, so she sat down and looked at it. Then she got up and dug under the perch until it fell. She picked up the bird and walked away. The ring slipped off the fallen perch, and she dashed into the woods. Clever isn't she?"

I am shaking my head and grinning at Alice.

"I was going to let the prairie falcon go, too," she goes on, "but a pickup with a camper on it came into the woods and I ran behind a big tree. Two men got out, saw that Frightful and one other bird were missing, and cursed a lot.

"They were real mad. When they saw the coyote tracks they decided she had killed both Frightful and the other bird. I guess they were afraid she would kill the last one, because they packed her up, gathered their gear, and left. I don't know who they were."

"They were thieves and they went to Beaver Corners, not far from here. The conservation officer arrested them this morning."

"They were arrested?" Her eyes are wide open and sparkling. "Well, that's good. I didn't like them."

"What's more, they killed the coyote and her pups."

"Oh, no, Sam," Alice puts her fingertips in her mouth, bites them, and takes them out. "Oh, no. The coyote was so nice. I wanted a puppy. What's the matter with people?"

"Some humans think we have the right to be the only predators on earth."

Frightful spirals down from the sky, throws up her wings, and hovers above my lifted hand. My heart pounds.

"Creee, creee, creee, car-reet."

"Hello, yourself, Frightful. Hello, hello."

She wants to come back. I can have her again. All I have to do is whistle her name and she will alight on my fist.

"Call her, Sam," Alice cries urgently. "Call her. Call her."

I purse my lips to whistle. That's all it will take—one whistle of three notes, down, up, down. I want her so much. Frightful "waits on," listening for her name, the signal for her to drop to my hand.

"Call her, Sam. Please, get her back."

I press my lips together. Frightful spreads her tapered wings and catches a rising thermal of spiralling air. She circles up and up and up. All I have to do is whistle. She's waiting for me to call her. She needs me as much as I need her.

She's at the top of the thermal, a speck in the sky. She waits. I don't whistle.

She tarries a moment longer, then peels off, and speeding like a falling star, shoots off into a cloud and is gone.

"Oh, Sam," Alice cries. "Why didn't you call her? She would have come back."

"Because," I answer softly, "she can breed. I saw her flirt with a tercel last spring. She will have young.

There will be wild peregrines on the cliffs again."

I take Alice's hand and squeeze it. "Thank you, for setting her free."

We stand on the escarpment for a long time, staring up at the cloud through which Frightful sped to freedom.

After a while we let ourselves down to our ledge and campsite. I sit on a rock with my head in my hands.

Alice hugs her knees. "Well, here we are," she says. "We don't have a peregrine, and you won't keep the baby goshawk, so it's a good thing I took Crystal with me."

"What do you mean?"

"When I started out to get the goshawk, I decided I might as well take Crystal. Mrs. Strawberry once said that the Monroe Farm near Livingstonville breeds Poland Chinas. Since the farm was on the way to the Helderberg Escarpment, I decided to drop her off."

I swallow hard as I recall the placard on the Monroe Farm.

"To be bred?"

"Well, we don't have Frightful anymore."

"Alice, that means piglets."

"Of course," she snaps. "She's not going to have falcons, that's for sure."

"I hate pigs, Alice," I say. "You know that. They rout up the forest floor and destroy the plants and the animals that live among them. They're smelly. . . ."

My tenderness for Alice is fading. I see my wilderness home muddy with wallows and stippled with pig bristles.

"Oh, Sam," she says. "I wouldn't bring her up on the mountain. I'll be keeping her in Mrs. Strawberry's empty pigpen."

"Thank you, Alice," I say and sigh.

Kneeling before the fire, I pull apart the coals and place the groundnuts in them.

"Hall-oo, the house!"

"Bando!" I shout and climb up to the top of the escarpment to greet him. The female goshawk drops down from her nest and, feet outspread, bombs Bando.

"Hey," he yells, dropping to the ground. "She's a wild one."

"Come down to our ledge where she can't see you," I say and lead the way.

The goshawk brushes me with her wing as I throw my legs over the escarpment and scramble down to our camp. Bando is close behind.

"Alice!" he shouts. "Where have you been? We've been looking all over for you."

"You should have known where I'd be, what with Frightful confiscated," she says sounding miffed, and then I know why. She starts telling him about the baby goshawk and how I won't keep her after all the trouble she has gone to.

"Sam's right," Bando says, and she sits down in a huff.

Eagerly I ask him what happened in Altamont.

"Bate, his buddy, and the Arab are free on bail pending trial," Bando says. "And the prairie falcon is on her way to Idaho.

"How's that for a happy ending?" he asks and takes a sandwich from his packbasket.

"We have a happier one," I say.

"What is it?"

"Frightful is free."

"She's what?"

"Free. Alice found her in the woods by the Rensselaerville waterfall and cut her jesses."

"You did?" he says, taking her hands in his. "Alice, you're wonderful." He looks at me.

"Do you think she'll survive?"

"I sure do. She was here only fifteen minutes ago, fat and beautiful."

"Frightful was here? How do you know?"

"I know all right," I say, looking at the sky. "She called my name."

Bando is grinning.

"That *is* the perfect ending," he says and, sitting down, looks out across the beautiful valley and mountains.

I pull a groundnut out of the fire, let it cool, peel it, and hand it to him.

"Here we go again," he says and, hesitatingly, takes a bite.

"Hey, this is darned good. What is it?"

"Pignut," I say, "for one of its many names." He laughs and takes another bite.

Later, as we all watch the sun slide down the western edge of the great escarpment, we sit in thoughtful silence. The stars come out. The moon is just rising, but it is so dark a daytime bird can't see. I get to my feet.

"It's time to take the little goshawk back." I put on Alice's work gloves and pick up the nestling.

Stroking her softly, I place her in Alice's backpack and scramble to the escarpment top. Gingerly I climb the tree, trying not to jar the little bird too much. Then, high above the waterfall, the woods, and the great wide valley, I nestle her among her siblings. They murmur a greeting and rouse. I think of the wild forests, the cliffs, and the meadows over which they and their offspring will reign, I hope, forever. Then I climb down.

The return of the little bird was as uneventful as her capture was frenzied. The parents, who were sitting in a nearby tree, did not move. They never saw me in the dark. I hope they can count to four. It would make them happy.

I drop back to our ledge, to find Alice balled up like a little caterpillar and sound asleep. Bando is stretched out on his back, his hands under his head, looking out at the stars.

"You know, Sam," he says when I sit down.

"What, Bando?"

"There's a miller in Rensselaerville who knows how to convert a water mill to electricity." He rolls his head my way to watch my reaction.

I see Frightful peeling off and vanishing from sight. I see the little goshawk cuddled against her siblings. I see the stars in their places and hear the waterfall shooting to its destiny out over the edge of the escarpment.

"I'll look into it," I say. "Zella and Alice would like it."

"What about yourself? Would you?"

"Yes. I'm ready. It will make them happy. Besides, I'm going to be very occupied. I'm going to speak to the conservation officer about getting a falconer's license."

"But Frightful's gone."

"You said your friend Steve needed people to raise and hack peregrine falcons. I'd like to do that."

"You're certainly qualified, and he's often said he would like to have someone raise the birds in a natural setting. He thinks they would adjust to the wild more easily." Bando frowns and turns to me. "But, Sam, won't it be hard to come to love them as you will, and then have to let them go?"

"You ask that, Bando, because you don't know what it feels like to set a peregrine falcon free."

```
J          George, Jean
GEO          Craighead

           On the far side of
           the mountain
```

$13.95

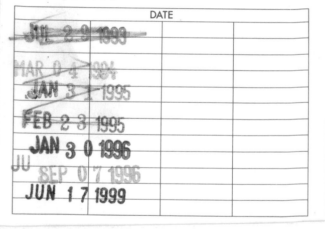

DATE		
JUL 2 9 1993		
MAR 0 4 1994		
JAN 3 1 1995		
FEB 2 3 1995		
JAN 3 0 1996		
SEP 0 7 1996		
JUN 1 7 1999		